shining
the light

a.s. coomer

ATLATL

Atlatl Press
POB 293161
Dayton, Ohio 45429
atlatlpress.com

shining
the light

For my brother, Ethan

contents

Introduction

Like all initial biographies, this will probably be more of an enshrinement than an objective look into the subject's life and art. Before a careful study is the unadulterated adoration for the art. Then, with time, comes the appreciation of the technique, of the craft. That being said, I've gone to the places I'm going to tell you about. I've sat down and interviewed the people you'll hear from in these pages. I've set aside my obligations, personal and professional, and completed a three-year odyssey to bring these words to life. And Alive I think they are. Alive with the Truth, the Way, the Light. Alive with the wolves at the door. Alive with the sad moon smiling down. Alive with the Darkness and the Shadow barely at bay. This is the life and death and art of Homer Antumbra.

Note: I will not hide my adoration for Homer Antumbra's work. Likewise, I will not hide when his artistic endeavors have fallen short or let me down. The idea of writing this biography on little known singer-songwriter Homer Antumbra came to me late in the winter of 2011. Homer had embarked on what would become his final tour and stories had reached me of his quickly deteriorating mental and physical health. Concerts became an hour and a half of improvisation. The songs previously recorded (and coveted and appreciated by too few) were nowhere to be found. Those songs had

1

left Homer. Instead, rambling ten-minute songs about the impending darkness, vast and complete, hovering just outside of view, the wolf-headed women and sharp-toothed men slipping in and out of the shadows at his heels, and the death lullaby from the sad-faced but smiling moon were what came through the PA.

It's too easy to write it all off as the rambling of a lunatic. The words of a crazy. Too easy and too myopic. The themes and motifs of what I've taken to calling Homer's End Sermons were there at the beginning too, when his mind was fresh and much less burdened by the years of travel and hard living, not to mention whatever hardwiring for self-destruction was already preprogrammed in there. His diary, written in his meticulous and shifting writing, sheds light on this. He had kept a diary since he was in his early teens. Written in one notebook until the pages were filled then picking up right where it left off in another.

At the time of his death, in the first days of spring 2012, he had filled a battered, leather and cardboard trunk nearly three feet deep and wide, full of these notebooks. Songs, poems, lyrics, stories, incidents: all there. Recorded on Greyhound buses, in the backs of passenger vans, seedy hotel rooms, barroom booths, the backrooms of venues, under overpasses. Everywhere and anywhere the word—the Truth—took Homer Antumbra he'd channel it and put it all down. Crazy it might sound to the uninitiated but enlightening and chock-full of experience and understanding it is to the student. With the grasp of background and familiarity with his life and art, the last shows reveal the final flickers of the candle, the Shining of Homer Antumbra, the last gasp of Light before the Long Dark.

No one in modern alternative music has done more for the sound and the craft than Homer Antumbra. His songs pushed the boundaries of storytelling, song structure and content through tonal paintings, blending together characters freshly wrought from his pen with themes as old as Sin. Pain, regret, loss, hope and struggle all fused into a cohesive cathartic experience as universal as the emotions themselves. Understanding Homer Antumbra and his music is understanding the self, the undercurrents swelling and raging in each of us.

This project has taken many forms since I started compiling all the materials together into one cohesive document. Originally, I had fictionalized the interviews into vignettes and scenes then interspersed them with the diary entries and lyrics but found it unappealing. Too much of the author in there. Then I laid it out with the interviews taking the lead but it wasn't as easy on my group of beta readers as I'd hoped. Lastly, in the form you now hold in your hands, is the transformation complete. The interviews are there. The diary entries are there. The fictionalized accounts of some of the interviews that were more powerful or poignant in scene and seen than by account. All of it is there. All of it is Homer. All of it is the Truth.

I will not give a track-by-track breakdown but I will highlight important themes and motifs in the albums and songs as well as those that indicate a particularly dynamic change or shift in artistic output. As with all musical biographies, a careful listen of the subject's music is key to a full understanding and appreciation of the artist. Sometimes it's not what you say but how you say it. The same goes for many of Homer Antumbra's lyrics. They must be heard to be fully apprehended for all their nuance and purport.

The book is broken up into three parts for a total of thirteen chapters. I've done my best to scrape together the most relevant portions of the interviews and have strived to keep as much of myself out of this as I possibly could. That being said, the emotional impact of the work described between the covers of this document is both crushing and enlightening, daunting and hopeful, and to completely minimize this impact would be detrimental to anything worthy of the man's name and art.

A.S. Coomer

As with any account based primarily on the word of others there will be differing of opinions and disagreement as to the facts, both large and small. I've tried to give everyone their rightful say but the reader would do well to keep in mind that this is the story of Homer Antumbra and his music, not necessarily about his every misgiving and flaw. We all have reasons for doing the things we do, for saying the things we say. I've done my very best to tell the Truth and Shine the Light on the Way.

Darren B. Harrison
Elizabethtown, KY
August 11, 2016

PART ONE

PORTRAIT OF AN ARTIST OF THE NIGHT & SHADOWS

Chapter One
The Chosen Must Walk

Right there. Right there—wait. Where'd he go? Slipped back into the Shadows. I swear I've seen him before. Swear it. Those blank, black-filled eyes, the gleam of those teeth even though there's no light to reflect . . . I've seen him before. He got on somewhere just outside Duluth and I've felt his eyes drilling into the back of my head ever since. I felt his wolf's teeth vibrating under his man-mask.

The snow crunches under my feet as I step off the bus. Crunch, Crush, Crunch. It must be weeks old. The swirling gray sky above tells me there's more coming. Guitar and valise in hand, I take off, all the while watching the bus over my shoulder. The door closes then the thing snakes away toward the interstate.

Didn't see him get off but not a second after the bus turns the corner I hear his steps, turn and see him slip nondescript back into the Shadows. I've seen him before. I swear it.

I find the alley quickly, can't remember how many times I've been here. Thirty-seven steps to the backdoor. Three quick strikes to the door with the valise and I hear the steps crush-crunching down the alley toward me. No point in looking, too much Dark-

ness, too many Shadows in the alley.

The door with the black raven's head opens and someone new stands in the light and din. Heat, laden with stale beer and the barroom chatter rush out, buffet me.

"You're late," he tells me and steps aside, holding the door for me.

I step inside and breathe a sigh of relief as the door closes.

From the PA, I hear the twang of an electric, fuzzed but not overloaded guitar amp, trembling with a heavy dose of tremolo. Major key and loud. My eyes adjust to the light and I walk past the doorman, who's busy telling me god-knows-what, on down the narrow hall to the backroom. I know my way. I can't remember how many times I've been here.

I open the case and tune my guitar. A beer appears before me. I run through a few chords, old ones with new melodies, scribble a few lines to something I've been carrying with me since Kansas City. Add the bit with the frozen steps and before that the eyes bright and teeth gleaming from the back of the bus. The man the man the man I've seen him before. The man is after me. I'm not completely sure he's real but I know he's after me. For what I've become. Everything I swore I would never be. Just like my father. Just like my father. Just like my father. Whether he's real or not doesn't matter, the man is after me.

Someone comes for my guitar for soundcheck. Another beer appears. I scribble some more into my diary until it is time to play. I am handed back my guitar and shown back into the narrow hallway. A fear grips me. The man is waiting. Those hungry eyes and gleaming teeth. The man is waiting for me amongst the waiting, watching, expecting faceless.

I see him plainly. Just as he is: part of the Shadow. I know he will be out there in the room. I will stand before him, armed only with the guitar, my voice and the Truth. With each step I take down the hall, my fear abates. I'm taking one more step along the

Way, then another, then another. I'm going to Shine the Light. The man may be waiting for me but I'm going to Shine the Light before I go.

I step out into the pale light and stand before the mic. I take off my glasses, leave them sitting on the amp. I let my left hand finger the chords and close my eyes. I can feel him watching. I can tell he knows what I am, what I turned my back on, the debt that must be paid. I keep my eyes closed and pick out the melody with my bare fingers. I feel the words before they come. I let them come. The man is here. The Truth is here too, though. The man becomes background, static. He can be forgotten for now. Telling the Truth is all that matters now.

—From Homer Antumbra's Diary

I first heard the music of Homer Antumbra in 2004. I was working for *Gatekeeper*, a now defunct independent magazine based out of Louisville that covered avant-garde poetry but occasionally had pieces on music and art. It was one of my first assignments and I was fresh out of grad school. I wasn't sent out to cover Homer Antumbra. In fact, I had no idea who he was before being handed the assignment. My editor was a huge fan of art-core act, Satchell Mariner, who I was sent to cover. They were headlining a three-night stand at the Louisville Palace with Homer Antumbra opening.

I decided to go to the first two nights and focus solely on the concert itself. I would get there early and watch the thing set up, catch the opening act then take detailed notes and photographs of Satchell Mariner. On the third night, I would interview the opener as well as headliner and get some backstage shots for the piece.

I really wanted to impress my editor. I didn't plan on writing for *Gatekeeper* for long and hoped to use the story as a launching pad for something more story intensive. I quickly secured all the recordings of Satchell Mariner and Homer Antumbra I could get my hands on and scoured them start to finish. I started with Satchell

A.S. Coomer

Mariner, as they were to be the main meat of the bit but couldn't find any connection to their music. Sure, they were talented but it just wasn't my cup of tea. The disconnected lyrics and dogmatic adherence to avoiding melody made them super trendy in the art world (especially at *Gatekeeper*) but nearly impossible to listen to on a repeated basis.

I popped *blackblacktheskywasblack* into my laptop for a much needed break from Satchell Mariner. From the opening chords, minor and slow, I was hooked. I stopped the CD, plugged in my noise-cancelling headphones, and restarted the album. The narrow confines of my cubicle disappeared and I found myself on a dark crossroad somewhere in rural, nighttime America. Everything was painted in silver and the shadows hummed with malevolence. From the deep blue night sky, the sad-faced moon smiled down at me, sending shivers racketing across my body. The Darkness swelled and I saw the wolf-headed stranger step out into the road before me. I entered the haunting world of Homer Antumbra for the first time.

Start to finish, *blackblacktheskywasblack* was the most gripping album I had ever heard. The first run through I just sat there in my uncomfortable chair and listened. I didn't take notes. I didn't read the lyrics. I didn't Google all I could about the artist. The music was too arresting for anything but to sit there, still as a rock, and let it wash over me like some midnight ice water baptism.

When it was over, I still just sat there with the headphones on and my eyes closed. I didn't want to do anything. I was still in that dark place, Shining the Light. I felt more engaged than I ever had after reading a really good book. I felt that I had partaken in the struggle between Light and Darkness. I had walked the road, hunted, and kept moving one foot in front of the other until I came to the end. That was what you had to do. It was that simple. You Shone the Light until it was out. I restarted the record and took out the booklet to go over the lyrics.

I didn't have long to delve into Homer Antumbra's music. My assignment—to cover Satchell Mariner's three-night stand at the Louisville Palace—was just three days away. When I approached my editor with the idea of focusing on Homer Antumbra instead of Satchell Mariner I might as well have been asking to go cover Bon Jovi or John Mellencamp. *Gatekeeper* was an art rag. We did A-R-T. Satchell Mariner was a collective of artists presenting their art in musical form to express the limited confines of the 2D medium. Blah blah blah.

So it went.

I went back to my cubicle and reread the band's lyrics and listened again to their songs. Nails on a chalkboard but it was my job. I learned all I could about the band, their history (mostly flunked out art school students), and pored through their lyrics looking for themes and motifs, of which there were negligible, forgetful, meaningless threads on being a black sheep, etc. To me it sounded like, "Yeah, my daddy paid for art school but it was just too narrow-minded there for the likes of me."

I studied up on Homer Antumbra too. In my free time, at home, and a little at the office. I found few interviews and fewer still in which the interview reached some sort of journalistic completion. The four I found ended abruptly and seemingly without anything other than the interviewees prickliness as a cause. Most of them were what you'd expect of small-town papers' interviews with unknown musicians. Full of questions along the lines of: Where do you come from? What kind of music do you play? If you had to compare yourself to another musician who would it be and why?

Homer Antumbra's answers were cryptic and veiled. Here's an excerpt from Des Moines' *Local Daily*:

LD: What genre would you consider your music?
HA: Religious. They're all religious songs.
LD: So, you're a Christian musician?

A.S. Coomer

HA: More of a gambler really. I know he's watching and I know I got a debt to pay.

LD: A gambler? Can you explain what you mean by that?

HA: You know or you don't. You tell the Truth or you don't. I can't help anyone right now.

He ended the interview at that point and the rest of the piece explained how the interviewer was unsure if he was being pranked or dealing with a crazy person. The interviewer didn't go to the show to find out what kind of musician he interviewed. Or if he did, there was no mention of the concert in the following weeks.

The other interviews I read went much the same way. I was determined to interview the man and get more out of him than these fools. They obviously had no idea who they were interviewing nor did they care to do any investigating prior to their assignments. Having heard the man's music, who on earth would give a shit about what genre of music the man thought he should be lumped into?

I found the contact information for the record label, Glow-In-The-Dark-Skeleton Records, on the back of *blackblacktheskywasblack* and began my interesting correspondence with label owner, Herschell "Hershey" Walters, which continued up until the completion of this manuscript. I arranged for an interview with Homer Antumbra to occur after the show on the last night of the mini-residency. Mr. Walters warned me that "Ant don't like interviews or interviewers." Ant, I learned, was what many of those close to Homer Antumbra called him. I thanked him for the warning and told him I'd make it brief and not take up too much of the man's time.

I'll spare the details of the assignment save for those related to the subject matter of this book. If you want to check out Satchell Mariner, you're more than welcome to but, in my opinion, they're not worth your trouble.

That first night I got there early and set myself up off to the right and waited impatiently for Homer Antumbra to take the stage, which he eventually did. The PA was blaring an old James Brown record, which stopped suddenly in mid-song, the house lights cutting off. A single spotlight shone down to the mic and Homer Antumbra walked out with his guitar strapped around his neck. He did not introduce himself, nor did he name the songs he played.

The raucous crowd was silenced by the intensity of the tall, slender man towering over them from the stage. He played for forty-five short minutes. In that time, he strung eight songs together. Eight songs with no pause or break between them, all intertwined and wrapped as tightly as lights on an overcrowded Christmas tree. He left no time for applause or response of any kind from the audience between the songs. Nor would they have known what to do if he had given them the chance. The few times I was able to pull my eyes off the magic man before me, I saw blank faces with wide eyes staring up at the ghostly figure on the stage. Drinks were held and I noticed their levels remained the same over the course of Homer Antumbra's set. Everyone appeared to be completely bemused.

When he turned and walked off the stage after the last note fizzled into sonic obscurity, no one applauded. They turned to those around them and resumed their drinking, laughing, talking, cursing, snarling. All the things they had been doing before those forty-five minutes of facticity transported them somewhere deep within themselves and away from the superficial trappings of the pseudo-intellectualism of Satchell Mariner and the crowd they attract. It was like some sort of collective amnesia related to some traumatic experience they were not capable of dealing with. I couldn't keep my mouth from hanging open.

I listened to the conversations around me and not one of them so much as mentioned what had just taken place before them. I turned to a brunette absorbed in her cell phone beside me and asked her what she thought of Homer Antumbra. She stared blankly at me and asked, "Who?"

I crossed the crowded room to the bar as Satchell Mariner took the stage. I drank the beer as they played through the first two of their jangling, clashing art-rock songs. I turned around and ordered another. While waiting for the bartender to come back with my drink, I saw Homer Antumbra at the far end of the bar, a bottle of beer and shot glass before him. He was scribbling in a notebook and taking sips from the bottle.

I watched him for some time, his back to the stage, the thick lenses of his glasses glinting in the lights from the stage, furiously engrossed in what he was doing. He abruptly slapped the pen on top of the page he had been working on and threw back the shot. Then his eyes found mine and honed in. There was no expression on his face. I didn't know whether to look away, smile and wave, or take my beer on down to the stage. Satchell Mariner decided for me.

Over the PA, I heard my name called. I noticed the band had stopped playing and lead singer, Bryce Trent, had the house lights turned on and was repeating my name.

"There's supposed to be a reporter from *Gatekeeper* here tonight to cover us. Darren Harrison, where are you? Darren Harrison?"

I stepped back into the crowd and weaved my way to the stage, holding my bottle of beer over my head. He pulled me up onto the stage and presented me to the crowd. I thought I could still make out Homer Antumbra at the bar but wasn't sure with the spotlight shining down on me.

I snapped a few shots of the band from the stage and hopped back into the crowd as the band played on. When I got back to the bar, Homer Antumbra was gone. The bartender saw me and slipped a bill across the countertop.

"He said you'd be picking up his tab," she yelled.

I picked up Homer Antumbra's bar tab for the second and third nights too. They weren't too bad as I found he did most of his drinking backstage, where the booze was free. He would've bankrupted me if I had to pay for every drink he'd taken but I didn't know that at the time.

His second night's setlist was completely different from the first. He didn't play one song from the previous night. On the third night, he played a mixture of the previous two nights' songs, seemingly the strongest combination of the songs that all interlocked and formed some hour-long melody. It sounded like a highway's subconscious—all motion, all movement, always leading somewhere else. Like the first night, after he finished playing, the crowds on the second and third nights held onto a moment's fleeting silence that suddenly erupted back into their total oblivion as their senses were returned to them.

I didn't approach Homer Antumbra at the bar during Satchell Mariner's set on either of those last two nights. I figured that if he wanted to talk to me before our scheduled interview, he would. Since he didn't, I let him be. He did raise his shot glass to me on the third night and nod his head in my direction. The bartender slid a shot before me and pointed down the length of the bar to where Homer Antumbra was closing his notebook and finishing his drinks. When I got the bill that third night it was significantly higher than it had been the previous two nights.

When the show was over, I met Homer Antumbra in the lobby of his hotel. We sat in the stiff leather armchairs in an uncomfortable quiet for a few moments after I mumbled through my thanks for allowing the interview and commenting on what great performances he had given the past three nights.

I had sketched out some questions I thought would engage him but sitting there with him the questions didn't feel right, having been scripted beforehand. I can't explain exactly why but it had something to do with the flow of things. I've interviewed Homer Antumbra dozens of times over the years since that first interview and have felt the same each time. Predetermining the questions of the interview or even remotely setting up the meeting as a Q&A felt like willing a stream into existence in the heart of a desert and deciding that it will flow uphill. It wouldn't happen and the whole thing would feel like the farce it was. It was a conversation that Homer Antumbra required. One on his terms and at his design and administration.

I threw my first few questions at him and he didn't respond. I felt panic rise but he didn't let me dangle too long. He cleared his throat and turned his eyes to me for the first time since we sat down.

"Why did you want to interview me?" he asked.

I thought about it. I couldn't tell him it was part of my job. It really wasn't. He wasn't part of my assignment really. He was to be summed up in a sentence or two, a paragraph at most. It wasn't because I thought he would give me the interview that would springboard me into another, better job either.

"You're overthinking it," he said.

"I heard your records," I told him.

Homer Antumbra nodded his head like this was an acceptable answer and, to be honest, it felt like the only right one.

"What do you want to know?"

I just barely stopped myself from saying 'everything' but only just barely.

Here before me sat a man who wasn't appreciated, wasn't known, and would never achieve anything beyond critical acclaim (and mostly from small-timers like myself). I asked some of the other people after his set on the second night what they had thought of the opener. The most I got out of anybody was: "He was good but a weird fit for a Satchell Mariner show." I couldn't agree more but for completely different reasons than the University of Louisville's Speed School student with dyed pink hair.

"Why do you do it?" I asked.

"Because I have to," he said. "I didn't have the whole say in the matter. Some things are chosen for you, predestined, but there're always choices to be made."

He spoke slowly but surely. These were obviously things he'd asked himself and asked himself often.

I let the words sink in. There were undercurrents there but I felt the waters were too deep for a first interview.

"Why are you working at *Gatekeeper*?" he asked.

The question caught me off guard but I answered because I felt an obligation to answer. It was a question my parents, my father particularly, had asked me a dozen times and one in which I had refused to give more than the most cursory of answers.

"I don't really know," I said. "It's not something I had ever really planned on. It just sort of, uh, happened."

He nodded.

I wanted to be able to tell him I deeply agreed with the artistic view of the magazine. That I felt a strong kinship with the readership. Something, anything, along those lines but the truth was that I simply didn't. I didn't read the thing myself. I did my job and wanted to impress but I couldn't've cared less about the avant-garde art world or the pompous pompadours and skimpy silk dresses that went along with it.

"Don't dwell on it. People and things have a way of blowing around."

He was right. I didn't stay with *Gatekeeper* for three months after that interview. And not six months after I left, the magazine closed down for good. Satchell Mariner also called it quits within a year of my first meeting Homer Antumbra.

"You read much?" he asked.

"Yes. A lot of nonfiction at the moment."

"Ever read Huang Mo?"

I shook my head.

"He wrote some really interesting things. I like his haikus best.

They're not what you'd expect."

I didn't know what to say. I hadn't read a haiku in my life that I could remember. I hadn't read poetry outside what had been required in AP English in high school. *Gatekeeper* was a weird gig the more I look back on it.

"'The chosen must walk. The road is covered in night. Nothing is as seems,'" he said.

"What?"

"That's one that's stuck with me over the years. Look, I got a few things to attend to. I've enjoyed talking with you. Let's keep in touch." He gave me his email address and left me standing in the empty hotel lobby.

I can't tell you how many drafts I wrote and trashed. It seemed like at least three times a week I'd type up an email to send to Homer Antumbra but hesitate on sending it and, upon rereading, would eventually send it only to my cyber trash can. I checked out a book of Huang Mo's verse from the public library and pored through that too. He was right, the stuff was very interesting, particularly the haikus.

I went down to ear X-tacy and picked up *thesesongsiforgot* and *whatwillcomewillcome*, which was all they had from Homer Antumbra. *thesesongsiforgot* was a five song covers EP containing old folk ballads from Dust Bowl and Great Depression era American history. The songs themselves were familiar to me but they were completely stripped of all semblance to the originals. In their place were sparse, organ-filled chants and whispers. It was truly captivating. The record played like the recording of a boxcar tabernacle pulling off into the night.

The other album, *whatwillcomewillcome*, was Homer Antumbra's second, the follow-up to *blackblacktheskywasblack*. This featured nine songs, all originals, all backed by a band. The tone was identical to its predecessor but the execution couldn't have been more different.

This was an all-electric, loud-soft-loud approach. All the lyrics were just as personal, just as strangling, but this time it seemed the emphasis was on making the band do the work. The songs were driven by Homer's Fender Telecaster, the pounding combination of Stephen Michael Harold's drums, Janice Angela Steinbeck's bass, and Skip Lewis' slide guitar and organ overtones. The thing played like a midnight thunderstorm.

A month passed and I finally crafted an email I sent off before I could erase. In it, I asked him what he was currently working on as well as what he'd been listening to lately. I also thanked him for introducing me to the work of Mo. He responded within a day.

"Working on a series of albums about a fellow traveler," he wrote. "Think of it as a Homeric *Odyssey* of sorts, no pun intended. I'm not really sure how many [albums] it'll end up taking to tell the whole story but it'll be more than three for sure."

This caught me off guard. The three recordings I had were anything but conceptual. They were personal, deeply so. I couldn't help but feel dismayed at the thought of Homer's music turning away and heading off in another—scripted—direction.

"I've been delving back into the Russian giants. Have you read *The Idiot*? It is probably my favorite from that time period. The older I get the more I come to respect the idea of the sanatorium," he wrote.

I hadn't read any of the Russians. I'd seen a movie based on *Anna Karenina* once but found its focus on societal life overbearing and tedious. I quickly went out and bought myself a paperback edition of *The Idiot* and set about reading it.

"As for what I've been listening to . . . the answer is: nothing new," he wrote. "I don't really pay attention to the happenings of the music world, what's popular, in fashion, etc. It's too distracting. I still listen to the same records I listened to ten years ago. They work for me. They keep things in perspective and I can start from the same point every day. There's so much change in my world each day that it helps keep me sane. For now. Yours truly, Homer Antumbra."

We kept up these periodic correspondences over the years, Homer dropping nuggets of wisdom along the way, as well as a wide and varied reading list, always things I'd never heard of or hadn't found the time to read. He kept me abreast of his doings and I went out and saw him every time he played within driving distance. The years passed quickly, it seems. I went through a series of menial jobs after leaving *Gatekeeper* and Homer went on to record an armful of incredibly dense records and relentlessly tour North America. I'll discuss the albums a little later on but next I'd like to move on to Homer Antumbra's early years.

Chapter Two

A Portrait of the Artist as a Young Man

"There truly ain't much all to do out here." The voice was aged, crackling like a dusty needle on a worn record. "No sir. You either work the mines, farm, drive a truck or join the army. That's it."

Just outside the porch in the blistering summer heat, the sky hung blue blue blue without a single cloud anywhere in sight. It was 2013 and I sat on Mary Ann Keaton's front porch, sipping from the homemade lemonade she was kind enough to make me.

"Homer wasn't going to have any of that. He wasn't much cut out for it."

The way she said 'for' purred out of her lipsticked lips as 'fur'.

"Never was much of a physical child. Didn't like to play football or basketball or even baseball really. No, Homer liked to read. Read more than anybody in his class. He was quite the writer too. Wrote some of the best poetry I'd ever read from somebody his age, he did. In fact, wait right here."

Mrs. Keaton disappeared into the darkness of her front door before I could say anything, leaving her rocking chair squeaking away on the rickety porch. The immensity of the geography was overwhelming and I stared out into the shimmering heat waiting on her to return. She lived a few miles outside Slalom and the nearest neighbor must've been five miles away. It was the quietest place I think I'd ever been. Just the faint rustle of sun-dried leaves and the occasional squawk of some miserable bird from the dead rose bush at the other end of the porch.

"Here it is, here it is," her voice preceded her out the door. The screen door slammed shut behind her and she handed me a rumpled piece of notebook paper with heavy creases. I unfolded it and read while Mrs. Keaton returned to her rocking chair.

"Wrote that in my class, yessir. Go on and read it aloud," she said.

"'Nightcrawler' by Homer Antumbra," I read. The rest read as follows:

> *Imagination stretches but horizon is always just over the rise;*
> *Always running, always inviting,*
> *Always calling, always singing.*
> *Those that flee, abandoned me;*
> *Always calling, always singing.*
> *The night sighs, the moon's sad smile and lonely eyes*
> *Cloudless and bare, frail wind drifting,*
> *Drifting forever across the darkened sky.*

I looked up from the paper at Mary Ann Keaton. She was nodding her head, her eyes closed and her mouth stretched tight across her wrinkled face, the chair bobbing slowly in the afternoon heat but making no breeze that I could feel.

"Told you. The boy could write now," she said, opening her eyes and reaching her hand out for the page. I acted like I didn't see her hand and reread the poem. The words, almost as smooth as the rocks on a river bottom. The same language, the same tone, the same longing ever present in Homer Antumbra's adult work.

I asked Mrs. Keaton if I could borrow the page, hoping she would offer it to me to have. She didn't. Mrs. Keaton declined, politely, and I settled for snapping a photo of the page sitting in my lap in the windless summer haze.

Looking back on the photo as I write this section, I notice that Mrs. Keaton had graded the work with what should've been an encouraging score of 98%. Reading the poem for the first and second times sitting on that oven-baked porch with Mrs. Keaton, I hadn't really paid attention to her marks. She wrote, "Excellent imagery" after the first line and "Musical" after line four. This should've encouraged the budding writer, though innocuously phrased in teacherese, but its effect was something Mrs. Keaton hadn't expected.

"He completely changed after this one," Mrs. Keaton said, taking back the paper. She carefully folded it and slipped it into a side pocket of her dress.

"What do you mean?"

"Well, I could see it on his face after I handed it back. His little brow furrowed and he looked stricken. That's the right word, now. Stricken." She nodded her head after repeating it. "I thought he was sick, see. So, I asked him what was wrong and he just shook his head a little and didn't really answer me. I didn't want to embarrass him in front of the whole class if he was sick so I moved on, returned the other students' poems. He didn't look good for the rest of the day."

I wiped sweat from my eyebrows and felt my shirt sticking to my back against the wooden swing. Mrs. Keaton didn't look the least bit uncomfortable, couldn't see a drop of sweat on her.

"I chose his poem to read at the end of the day. I always chose one of my kids' pieces to read at the end of the day. Kind of like positive reinforcement for expressing themselves articulately and creatively. I asked him to bring it up to my desk, which he did, then I had him stand beside me while I read it. He squirmed and looked downright uncomfortable the whole time. When I finished, I smiled down at him and asked the class 'wasn't that nice?' and he bolted. Straight fled out the door." Mrs. Keaton shook her head. "I made to chase after him but the bell rung and I figured what's the use."

"Do you think he was sick? Or do you think it embarrassed him having you read his poem?"

"I don't think he was sick. I didn't get the chance to ask him though. If I had to guess, I'd say it embarrassed him hearing those words he wrote read aloud. They had another poem assignment due the next day and the one he turned in was completely, utterly different than anything else he'd ever turned in."

"How so?" I asked. "Did you keep it too?"

"No. I didn't keep it. Wasn't worth keeping. It was drivel. Lifeless drivel. There was nothing in it. Nothing. I can't even tell you what it was about."

She was the poster child of the disappointed teacher. Her tight mouth turned down slightly at the corners and her head continued its minute shaking from left to right.

"What was so bad about it?"

"There just wasn't anything there. Like he didn't try. Sure, there were words there, more than the other poems he'd turned in, if I can recall correctly, but the words didn't do anything. There were images. No poetic devices. No energy."

"Why do you think he changed?"

"I still don't know."

Homer Antumbra continued to write but he largely turned away from poetry after Mrs. Keaton's reading of *Nightcrawler*. She didn't keep anything else he turned in. She said she called his mother about the drastic change in his writing but wasn't able to garner more than an "oh" from her. It seemed to Mrs. Keaton that Lillian Antumbra wasn't too worried about her son's writing and creative expressions. Mrs. Antumbra established that Homer was performing academically up to par and not causing any trouble and left it at that.

"He retreated into himself," Mrs. Keaton said. "I mean more so than he had before. A few weeks later, he came up to me after class after all the other students had left. He asked me if I might have 'mis-wrote' on his poem. He asked me if I really thought he was musical and I told him that of course I did. I told him that the structure of his sentences and the flourishing words almost took on a musical quality. I told him that and he just stared at me, blankly. I asked him if there was anything bothering him and it took him a moment to say anything. Then he asked me if I thought the things he'd been turning in since 'Nightcrawler' had been musical. I didn't want to hurt his feelings but I don't believe in lying to my students. I told him that no, I didn't think what he'd been turning in as of late was musical. He dropped his shoulders and sighed. I thought I had hurt his feelings but he said 'thank you' and took off before I could get anything else from him.

"I was worried about him so I took him out into the hall the next morning and talked to him. I told him that I thought he was a really talented writer and could go to college and become a poet. He seemed to like the idea but I could tell he didn't believe it could actually happen. He said he had his mother to look after and he couldn't leave her alone and go off to college. I told him that his mother was an adult and would be happy to see him get a college degree. He didn't seem to believe me. I let it go. What can you do?"

I shook my head. I didn't know.

"Well, he started missing school," she said. "He missed three days in a row and I called up his mother. She said she would 'handle it'. That day after school, I stopped off at Plumly's Filling Station for some gas and there he was."

"Homer?"

"Yep. He had started working there, filling up cars, cleaning up the windshields, airing up tires and all that. I asked him if this was why he was missing school and he said it was. He said his mother had worked out an agreement with Principal Dolland and he would be working at the filling station two days during the week and attending school just three. Of course, I didn't like this one bit but they were just starting to push career exploration and learning trades in the district and there was nothing I could do about it."

"What about his writing?" I asked.

"His writing got really . . . weird," she said and frowned. "I didn't care for it at all. He started writing these story poems. All about restlessness, desolation. They were sparse. There was no flowery language. There were no adverbs, no metaphors at all really. They were populated with these half-human, half-monster creatures, all animal heads with glowing eyes and fangs. They were hunting and hunted, killing and being killed. That's all it was. It was awful. I tried to talk to him about it but he bucked. Flat out wouldn't change what he was doing. Then he dropped out of school altogether at the beginning of his senior year and started working full-time down there at Plumly's."

The Red Lady—Lady in Red

> *Body of an angel but with a wolf's head.*
> *Standing in the road—the road that parts,*
> *Weaving the strings that bind my heart.*
> —From "The Red Lady"

> *The road parted there under the pale moonlight.*
> *Under the skeletal branches of a decaying sycamore,*
> *The wolf-headed woman in red waved, spoke*
> *And nothing was ever the same again.*
> —From "The Red Lady #2"

"Om, everybody called him that except Lillian, his momma—she called him Home. Just *Home*. You know like where you live,"

Janice Stewart said. "Anyway, Om didn't really run up and down the street like the other kids. He wouldn't really even play all that much, even when his mother signed him up for the peewees. He'd sit on the bench there and watch the clouds go by. Like he wanted to be a bird and just fly along with them. Fly along outta here. You could almost see it you know."

I met Mrs. Stewart in the basement of Slalom Baptist, where she was getting things ready for Sunday dinner.

"One time," she said, "I even saw him hunched over a book down there in the dugout. Wayne Nelson, Coach Nelson as the kids knew him, had to holler at him twice to pull him outta it and take the field. They stuck him out in right field, hoping nobody would hit anything his way." She slipped her hand into an oven mitt and pulled a bubbling dish, some sort of potato casserole, from the small oven.

"I don't think the boy could ever see all that well. Popfly after popfly he'd miss. Wayne would nod his head when Om would come dragging his feet into the dugout mumbling that he lost the thing in the sun. Even if it was cloudy!" Mrs. Stewart chuckled and set the casserole down on the stovetop. "Cloudy and he'd blame it on the sun and Wayne would just nod his head and nod his head again whenever Om would strike out. He always struck out too."

Janice Stewart lived on the same road as the Antumbras, two houses down, at the corner of Yates and Main on the outskirts of Slalom proper. She still lived there but her social schedule and my traveling itinerary didn't align for more than the quick thirty-minute interview I got just after Sunday service.

"Om was different. Not like serial killer different, I don't want you to get that impression. He was just quiet, to hisself. *Always* to hisself," Mrs. Stewart said.

"What do you remember about his mother and his home life?" I asked.

She leaned back against the oven and seemed to be thinking

back.

"You know, Lily wasn't much for socialization neither. I don't think I ever really said more than ten words to her at a time and, Lord knows, it was probably me doing most of the talking." Mrs. Stewart let the cackle loose again. She must've been old back when Homer was still avoiding the other neighborhood children.

"She wasn't rude or anything like that. She just kept to herself, you know? If she was invited to a get-together, she would go but she wouldn't stay any longer than was polite. It just wasn't her. But she wasn't stuck up. I don't recall her ever having any male friends, now that I think about it." She paused and looked up at me with a wry smile. "It's a small town, Mr. Harrison. Word like that spreads, you know? Anyway, I don't recall ever knowing that she had anybody stay over. Can't recall ever hearing about her going out on a date neither."

"What do you know about Homer's—Om's—father?" I asked.

Her smile quickly tightened and thinned out.

"You heard of Fox Grayson and the Disgrace, right?"

I shook my head. I hadn't.

"Lord, you're in for a real treat," she said. Something in her tone told me that if my morals were up to code I would think Fox Grayson and the Disgrace were anything but a treat.

Unfortunately, at this point it was time for Slalom Baptist's Sunday dinner and I wouldn't get to do any research into Fox Grayson and the Disgrace for some weeks. I'll return to this subject a little later on.

"Om was a weirdo. A dork. Always reading. Always scribbling away in his little notebooks. He'd make real good grades too. Teachers loved saying that we should all be like him. Then came high school." Nick Rooney had a nasally laugh, high-pitched and obnoxious. He responded to an ad in the *Slalom Weekly* I had put out about Homer Antumbra. I met him at Bob's Tavern, where he worked as a cook.

"But I guess that happens to a lot of people. In high school, the only thing he stayed great at was English. Still kept reading and scribbling. Stopped playing ball, thank God. He truly was awful. We'd see him down at Plumly's. He'd check the tires, clean the window, fill the tank up, check the oil, the whole deal. He'd do it like a machine. I remember some of the kids from school would try and get him riled up but never could. He'd ignore the remarks and go on about his business. He'd say 'please' and 'thank you' and was polite as you could get. I think people tried to push his buttons because they didn't understand him. He was different. Nobody was supposed to be different. Not like that," Mr. Rooney said. He was noticeably intoxicated, his face flushed.

"[The other kids] used to say that he must've thought he was better than everybody else, refusing to participate like he did. Wouldn't play sports, wouldn't joke around with the rest of us, wouldn't go to any of the dances, or to the movies we'd all go see. I mean I saw him at the Starry Night once but he was coming out of a matinee of *To Have and Have Not*, you know, the old Humphrey Bogart picture. Hey, you want to grab a drink?" he asked.

"No thanks. I don't really have a lot of time," I lied.

"The Starry Night had old-timey matinees like that. A lot of old people used to go see 'em. I think that's the only time I saw him and I was there just because my grandma was in town and she wanted to go see some old movie she said I just *had* to see. I heard that he went to a lot of them old-timey matinees though. Used to tease him that he was stuck out of time. Wasn't in the right place. Born in the wrong time, in the wrong town, in the wrong state, wrong country probably. He'd just look at me with the most serious face and nod his head. That's the most of an answer I could get outta him. Fucking weird, right?" He laughed and asked again if I wanted to go someplace else for a beer or two.

A.S. Coomer

I got Candice "Candy" Hewitt's name from Janice Stewart. Mrs. Stewart said there was some happening with the Antumbras there at the church she couldn't 'rightly recall' and for me to contact Candy Hewitt to get the scoop. I looked her up in the county phonebook and offered to buy her dinner down at Mel's, an old-school diner downtown.

Candy Hewitt had been the Sunday school teacher at Slalom Baptist during the several years the Antumbras attended services. When I told her Janice Stewart thought she might have a story to tell me, she started right into it.

"Om [had] come out of Sunday School—he must've been six years old then—just a-singin'. He always had such a beautiful voice. You should have heard him then too. 'Fore he got all mopey. Never did understand any of that." Ms. Hewitt smiled wanly and shrugged her shoulders. "Anyway, we'd had a real good Sunday School session and he'd come out singing some silly song that he heard on the radio somewhere or heard from one of the other children, *not* from me or the songs we sang at Sunday School.

"It was something about [starts singing] 'I'm a-goin' fur eh ride on the hayride. I'm a-goin' fur eh ride on the hayride. Come along, sing along, while we a-ridin' on the hayride.' I know I don't got much a voice now but Lord could I sing back then," Ms. Hewitt said and laughed. A very musical laugh to match her pleasant singing voice. "Anyway, we were walking up the stairs from the basement, where we had Sunday School, and Om was singing that song and bouncing around, dancing. Lily—that was Om's momma—was walking down the aisle before we even made it to the top of the stairs. Her face was redder than any tomato I've ever seen. Her lips were tight and white though. She grabbed Om by the arm and squatted down on her haunches. She looked him square in the face and told him that she couldn't believe he'd be singing the Devil's music right there in church. The Devil's music she called it! That silly song about a hayride.

"I tried to tell her that it was all right and that he'd been singing so pretty down there in the basement but she jerked him away without another word. She practically drug him out the front door and that was the last time I'd heard Om sing anything outside the hymnal until someone brought me one of his CDs . . ." Her words trailed off and she looked embarrassed.

"After his mother got on to him about the hayride song, Om's singing in Sunday School got very serious. He'd sing the songs with a look of concentration unlike any of the other children. I thought it was both cute and sad. Cute that he was trying so hard, and he was doing quite well, and sad because it seemed like he was trying to make up for the sin of singing that silly song. It wasn't my place but I really wanted to have a talk with Lily about that. But it wasn't my place and I didn't."

I had one more person to talk to while in Slalom. I drove out of town on Main and stopped at Plumly's Filling Station. A younger man, probably a high school student near to graduation, filled up my rental car, checked the pressure in my tires and cleaned the dust off my windshield. I asked if Marcus Plumly was around. I was told he was inside, in the back office. After explaining why I wanted to ask him some questions about Homer Antumbra and briefing him on his musical career, Mr. Plumly agreed to talk to me.

Mr. Plumly remembered Homer as hardworking but prone to daydreams and staring off into space for extended periods of time.

"He'd be right there checking the pressure of a customer's tires," Mr. Plumly said, "and a few minutes would go by and you'd turn around to see what was going on, whether the tires were done or not, and Om would be down there on his knees just looking off with his eyes all dazed and glazed. I'd shout at him, 'Om! Where's your head at, boy?' and he'd snap back into the here and now and finish up the tires, clean the windshield off, and apologize profusely."

I sat in a small, uncomfortable plastic chair across the desk from the man in his office, a dusty, enclosed room just bigger than a closet in the back of the filling station. A thin path had been made to the desk from the door amidst the boxes of candy bars and cases of soft drink cans. I had to step over a heap of what appeared to be some *People* magazines from last year that had either been forgotten about or just hadn't made the rack at Plumly's just yet.

"When there was nothing going on at the station, Om'd be sitting back there on the stool with his nose in a book. I'd seen him read all kinds of stuff: funny books, books of poetry, novels by some Ruskies, holy books from China or thereabouts, and books on mechanics, woodworking, you name it." Mr. Plumly's tone was not one of appreciation for a wide-ranging literary diet. "Now, don't get the impression that he neglected his work or anything like that. I guess that some people are just prone to daydreaming. It's in their makeup, their nature. But he was a hard worker. He went above and beyond the call of duty, you could say. He'd draw out maps for customers trying to find their way out of Nebraska while avoiding Oklahoma or Kansas. God, would people drive hours upon hours to avoid Kansas."

His laugh was deep and genuine.

"But you can't avoid that country. You have to either drive across it or fly over it. It's a part of the country. I remember Homer would tell people to do it at night. Said it was better that way. Just you and the stars, running down the horizon. That always stuck with me."

Chapter Three
S e a r c h   f o r   t h e   F o x

Homer Antumbra was born in Slalom Regional Hospital to Lillian "Lily" Antumbra in Slalom, Nebraska on January 21st, 1973. No father was listed on the birth certificate. That being said, from all accounts, including Homer's, Jayson 'Fox' Grayson was his father.

"He was my father," Homer Antumbra said. His straight answer to my question took me off guard. I was talking to him inside his room at Greystone in early 2012. I'd been visiting him once a month and our visits usually entailed listening to Homer ramble about anything and everything, sense and nonsense, and trying to glean what little substance from it I could. I'd told him several times that I was thinking about writing a piece on him. I had no clue it would become a full-fledged biography at that point and had taken to asking him questions about his past, including his early childhood, which was a subject we had never broached during our few years of correspondence.

I had asked him about Jayson 'Fox' Grayson and Homer had answered me. I didn't want to derail his train of thought so I sat in anticipating silence for him to continue.

"You know I never met him. Just heard momma talk about

him. Never went looking for him neither," he said.

This was a thought that hadn't occurred to me until that point. Homer Antumbra's saying he'd never sought out his father felt like a falsehood and, as if he was covering up his break with telling the Truth, Homer picked up the toy keyboard and started a dirge-like foxtrot.

I made some phone calls, searched the internet, made some more phone calls, eventually stumbling onto Jayson Elliot Grayson's March 22nd, 2009 obituary from a small county newspaper in northwest Arkansas. Mr. Grayson died in Eureka Springs, a quaint little city in the Ozark Mountains, from "natural causes" at the age of sixty. There were no survivors listed in the article.

The coroner's office had received a phone call from the police asking them to come claim the body of a deceased elderly man. Upon further investigation, the man's identity and age were established. According to the coroner's report, which was unusually informal, the deceased "looks much older than his age." For a coroner to say that of a corpse, one that had been dead for several hours according to the report, seemed significant. It'll seem even more so after we learn a little more about Jayson Grayson.

Born in small-town, southwestern Georgia, Jayson Grayson dropped out early on in high school and hit the road. He's got a police record in just about every state I've cared to look. Mostly for drunk and disorderly, disturbing the peace and the like, but on a few occasions there were incidents of assault and battery and two separate charges of theft by deception as well. He seemed to have picked up playing the guitar and the fiddle at an early age and had set out to make his living as a musician, playing roadhouses, bars, hotels, any and every gig he could get, with or without a band.

Seems he never set any firm roots down in any one place but had women in different parts of the country who'd take him in for convalescence for extended periods. There were more rumors of children fathered by Jayson Grayson than I had time or energy to follow up on. After nearly two decades of ceaseless travel and playing, Jayson Grayson had solidified a group of musicians that came to be known as the Disgrace.

"They called us a disgrace this one time at a club in Johnson City, Tennessee. See, we were playing at this real rowdy club off the interstate. We'd never played there before and the place was new. We got picked up to open for some yuppie singer from Nashville but we ended up beginning and ending the night. See, the audience had a way of interacting with us and the kind of songs we played. And this was the place's grand opening so the drinks were cheap. I mean dirt cheap," Nelson Daugherty smiled as he said it, the crow's feet at the corners of his eyes spidering out into a network of delta-like wrinkles.

"They about burned the place to the ground the second time we played 'Three Shots for Love'. Fox was up there just a-drinking with the best of them too. He always would. Well, the fire got started. The police came and the club owner, this real uppity prick, said we were no country band. He said we were a disgrace. Fox loved that. So, we just started going by Fox Grayson and the Disgrace," Nelson Daugherty said.

Nelson Daugherty is the last remaining member of the Disgrace. All the other band members have died—natural causes, cancer, murder, or of issues related to substance abuse. Nelson Daugherty had been a member of the group for years prior to the namesake incident and is still alive and making music at the time of my writing this. I spoke to him at his apartment in Charleston, West Virginia.

"Why'd they call him 'Fox'?" I asked.

"For a couple of reasons. One: he looked like one." Mr. Daugherty, who insisted I call him Nelson, showed me a picture of the two of them some thirty-five years earlier. Both men's mouths were carved into sly slits of grins and their eyes flashed in what must have been the glassy reflection of the camera's flash. "Two: he had a way of starting trouble. Starting trouble and, more often than not, finding a way to have someone else take the fall. Sly like the fox so we called him Fox."

When I asked Nelson what kind of trouble he was referring to he gave me a wry smile and said, "Some things that the statute of limitations haven't yet come up on," and would go no further.

Fox Grayson and the Disgrace recorded a few singles. They never got around to recording a full-length album. The labels their singles came out on have since folded and the songs themselves have not survived into the digital age. Sales were less than enthusiastic. They sold enough at their shows to warrant pressing a few hundred more but there was no mention of the singles in *Billboard* and no Grammy nominations or anything remotely of that sort. You can't find them on iTunes or Amazon. I was lucky enough to get to listen to a few of their 45s Nelson Daugherty had safeguarded over the years. The records themselves were not of the best quality—a thin vinyl, the grooves ground down from years of use—and neither was the quality of the recordings. The songs sound vaguely as if they were recorded in a barroom bathroom, which in all honesty, would fit with the songs' themes and subject matters.

The records I listened to were mostly cover versions of someone else's songs. They covered Hank Williams, Roy Acuff and the like. The only original song they recorded was their "hit" song: "Three Shots for Love," a song they played at every show for decades. This song was a drinking song. A drinking song that required audience participation (drinking) and that, I think, is the key to its relative level of success.

I called up Janice Stewart down at Slalom Baptist and asked her some more questions about Fox Grayson and the Disgrace and she provided me with a few names and numbers for more information. I spoke with several people regarding the band and their live performances—Slalom was a yearly stop for the band on their circuit—and have combined them for brevity into a conglomerate interview under a single fictitious male and female, Stewart Johnson and Angela Paterson, respectively.

"Tell me about a typical Fox Grayson and the Disgrace performance, Mrs. Paterson."

"Oh, it was such fun. That Fox was as handsome as could be. Had a real pretty voice and the band was tight too," she said.

"What, exactly, was fun about them?"

"Well, they played a lot of old-time country and western songs. They were funny too. Had these little jokes they'd do between the songs. Bantering, like, between the members of the band and Fox. All self-deprecating and whatnot," she said.

"You knew exactly what you were getting yourself into when you went out to see the Disgrace," Mr. Johnson said.

"And what was that?" I asked.

"You were going out to dance your ass off, drink, try and find a date for the night if you didn't bring one, and drink. Did I mention drink?" Mr. Johnson laughed.

"They played songs that we all knew and could sing along with. We loved that. Sometimes, we'd go out to see a band or a singer and they'd only play songs they wrote themselves or songs that no one had ever heard before. We didn't much care for that. Where's the fun in that?" Mrs. Paterson said.

"I can't tell you how many times I went out to see Fox and the Disgrace play in Slalom over the years," Mr. Johnson said. "I don't think I took the same girl more than twice either. There's no telling how much ass the Disgrace got me. I mean, they came out at least once a year. Two or three times in the year, more often than not, and I got laid nearly every single time. That's why 'Three Shots for Love' is still my favorite song of all time, well, next to 'Night Moves' by Seger anyway."

"Oh, I just loved that song. It was crazy though. Absolutely crazy. Shawn, my husband, used that song on me every time the Disgrace would come through town. He'd get me all liquored up and off we'd go," Mrs. Paterson said. Her smile was large and not a shade over half-embarrassed.

"Why are you blushing?" I asked her.

"Well, you know it makes me sound like some sort of floozie or drunk, saying it like that. I mean, the song can't be longer than four minutes and in it you're doing three shots of hooch," she said. "One of which, you're getting from someone that wants to be your lover that night."

The recorded version of the song that Nelson Daugherty played for me on his nearly ancient but in immaculate shape Thorens TD-124 turntable came in at three minutes and forty-five seconds. In it, the listener (or audience member, if you were at the show) was to take three shots, assumedly, of hard liquor. One for Fox, one for the listener and one for the listener's prospective lover.

"He said the same thing, the same script, before and during that song that he said for the entire twenty-five years we played it together," Nelson Daugherty said and chuckled. "We'd try to end our first set and our encores with it because it was so popular and interactive. [Fox] would say, 'This next song is for everybody. Every single person in this here establishment. We all want love. We all need it. This song is about loving yourself and, hopefully,' and then he'd pause and laugh before continuing, 'someone else a little later on in the evening.' The audience, even the ladies in the crowd, would all bust out laughing along with him.

"The initiated [those that had seen Fox Grayson and the Disgrace before and knew the procedure for the song] would already be making their way to the bar to buy the three shots for themselves and the three shots for their prospective lover. Some of the more popular gals would have six or nine shots lined up at their tables. Some of 'em would even do all nine!"

"I think I've seen [Fox Grayson and the Disgrace] play five or six times and every time they played that song it was like a mass exodus of folks, mostly men, to the bar," Mrs. Paterson said. "The first time I saw it, I was so confused. Nobody'd told me what to expect so I thought the show was over but the band stayed right up there on the stage so I thought everybody must've been gettin' sick of 'em. This was weird because I thought they were doing such a good job and I was having such a good time. Then Fox Grayson would go into the 'Three Shots' speech that he did every time I saw them play that song then and there after, and I understood what everybody in the audience was doing."

"While everybody was coming back with their hands and arms full o' shot glasses, Fox'd say, 'Now this song involves a little bit of what you might call 'audience par-tish-ah-pate-shon. I see several of y'all have seen me play a time or two and are already making your way to the watering hole. Good. For those of you that don't know' (Fox went through all of this even the first time he played the song with the band) 'you fellers need to go buy three shots of whiskey, preferably bourbon, for yourself and three more for that special someone who's got your eye tonight,'" Nelson Daugherty said.

"Now, most of the barkeeps already had a long line of shot glasses filled by this time in our set. I heard 'em call 'em 'Disgrace shots.' I knew one place in Charlottesville [Virginia] that had Disgrace bottles they'd make up when we were coming to town. Said they'd take the last bit of several whiskey bottles and combine them in a Four Roses bottle, that was one of Fox's favorites, until they got about a third full then filled the rest with water and did the same with another bottle.

"Of course, they charged regular price for these Disgrace shots. This kindly ticked me off the first time I heard about it but then I'd see a handful of people puking their guts out in the crowd while we finished the song and I got over that real quick."

"There'd be a flood of shots at Fox Grayson's feet by the end of that song. Men and women alike would buy him drinks during the set but the women would make it look like a Catholic church votive candle rack of whiskey at his feet during 'Three Shots,'" Mr. Johnson said. "They'd set down the shots [in front of Fox Grayson] with napkins under 'em after they scribbled their phone numbers or hotel room numbers or even their blasted addresses on 'em."

"When it looked like about everybody had made it back to their places with their shots, Fox would go on," Nelson Daugherty said. "He'd say, 'Now during the first chorus of this song, I'll take me a shot here myself. That's your cue to take one your own selves. Now the second chorus, I'll take me another shot but this one ain't for me. It ain't for you neither. It's for love in general. You have to celebrate the thing or it could very well die out. And nobody wants that. Can you imagine a world without love?' There'd be a chorus of 'Hell no's and the like from the crowd then he'd say, 'And the last chorus you find the one that's got you looking tonight and you take that shot staring di-rect-ly into their eyes. If they're feeling the same, they'll take their shot looking into yours.' There's no telling how many babies came as a result of that damn song." Daugherty's paunch jiggled with laughter. "We tramped all over this country, Fox acting as some drunken Johnny Appleseed or Country Swing Stork."

The show put on by Fox Grayson and the Disgrace was very much in the vain of performers such as Hank Williams, a mixture of comedic effect—mostly through self-deprecation that was more than likely wholly theatrical—and honed, well-crafted setlists. The songs played were specifically chosen to meet the demands of the audience of the night. The setlists evolved every bit as much as the scenery as the band made their way, crisscrossing the country on their honky-tonk circuit. Eventually, the setlist might contain only a handful of the same songs played at the start of a tour. Charlottesville, North Carolina's setlist was in stark comparison to Slalom, Nebraska's setlist. In this way, Fox Grayson was a forerunner in the niche market that would soon be perpetuated into mass acclaim by the likes of Sonny Stephenson and Black Jack Garrote.

But, according to Nelson Daugherty, there was much more to Jayson 'Fox' Grayson than just the barroom anthems.

"Fox would always have his guitar on him, always playing and singing and writing songs—most of which never found their way into the act. There would be slow, sad, melodic ballads of loss and love and I tried many a-times to get Fox to play them during the show or at least record 'em because they were better than anything we were doing—I mean *anything*—but Fox never would. He kept them close to him like they were something too personal, like his musical diary or something.

"There were some weird tunes in there too. Songs about animals and people fighting or stalking each other. Like some medieval knight's song or something. Valor and courage facing the dragon, you know? Always a shadow in the songs, or some such darkness. Fox was obsessed with it. One time he got good and real drunk, three days of straight drinking without a wink of sleep, and started playing this real sad song, tears coming down his cheeks, singing so softly that he was bringing more darkness into the world than light, how he hoped the Lord would forgive him and give him a place in the sun when he went. 'Bout to broke my heart. Sobered me up quicker than anything has in my entire life. Jail didn't even do it that fast."

Fox Grayson knew his audience. He knew the band's reputation and he knew the songs they could get away with. He didn't mess with the formula. It's unlikely he ever recorded these other songs, the songs Nelson Daugherty heard him play and tried, unsuccessfully, to get him to play live or record. I have been unsuccessful in finding any such recording. The dozens of people I interviewed about the Disgrace concerts never mentioned any songs on an emotional level as the ones described by Mr. Daugherty. The need for nearly constant movement and the drive to make music were two things Homer Antumbra very much inherited from his old man.

Chapter Four

The Commitment
(or The Commitment Broken)

Working fulltime at Plumly's, Homer Antumbra earned money, read widely, and listened to the radio, which Marcus Plumly always had playing. Away from the reaches of his puritanical mother, Homer could listen without reprisal to the rock and roll songs, the country songs, the pop songs, anything and everything that came through the speakers. He heard songs ranging from Tracy Chapman's "Fast Car" to U2's "Desire", Rod Stewart's "Forever Young" to Phil Collins' "Two Hearts", Morrissey's "Suedehead" to Bobby Brown's "My Prerogative" and countless others. It's hard to quantify just how monumental this was for Homer's development. He learned the value of hard work, the teachings of the literary masters, as well as the possibilities of song.

The Antumbras attended church every Sunday as well as the Wednesday night services when Homer was not working. Lily Antumbra was devoted. She read from the Bible daily and prayed both in the morning when she woke and at night before she slept. She did her best to instill this religiosity in her son.

A.S. Coomer

"They were there [Slalom Baptist Church] every Sunday," Candy Hewitt said. "And Lily was there every Wednesday evening too. She was quiet and intent. She listened to every word of Preacher Case's sermons and had private prayer meetings with him before and after the services on occasion. I think she was a good Christian woman. Hard but well-meaning."

"What about Homer?" I asked.

It took her a few moments to respond.

"I think he took to the stories. He liked to sing too," she said.

Years later, Homer Antumbra was interviewed by an alternative music magazine, now defunct, called *Night'n Gale*. He had just come off a tour with a Christian rock band, which confounded a lot of the people that knew Homer's music and listened regularly. The interviewer took the accusatory tone of the teenage youth he probably was and poked at Homer as if he were betraying himself and his music through the tour. Here's a sample of the interview:

Interviewer: Touring with [band name removed for legal reasons]. Wow. That's, like, weird, huh? You a Christian musician now?

HA: I'm trying to Shine the Light.

Interviewer: Do you play Christian songs now?

HA: They're all religious songs. Every one of them.

"Were there any stories that he favored over others?" I asked Candy Hewitt.

"Anything related to Good fighting Evil. That was what it all seemed to break down to for Homer. Good versus Evil. I think that's what he means when he's talking about the Light and battling the Dark or the Shadows." Ms. Hewitt took a sip from her coffee before continuing. "I don't think it ever really mattered what label you put on it for Homer. God, Jesus, whatever. Good was Good. Light was Good. I think church was just another way of looking at the evergoing battle between the two most fundamental forces of the universe."

Homer sent off several poems and short stories to various magazines across the country during this time period. This is known only through the several rejection notices he kept. Most were standard stock, templates printed and mailed off without so much as a gracing signature from the editor or slush pile reader, but there was one that warranted a handwritten reply. The subject line of the rejection letter read, "in re: Slipping." This piece has never surfaced but the editor commented that the poem was "searchingly beautiful but not a right fit for us right now." Homer was encouraged to "keep up the good fight but dress up the language."

Early into his senior year of high school, prior to turning eighteen years old, Homer Antumbra suddenly left Nebraska. He just left. There were no elaborate goodbyes. No two-week notice turned in at Plumly's Filling Station. No one to say goodbye to, really, other than his mother, Lily, but it's unclear whether or not he even did that.

"He killed his mother when he left like that," Janice Stewart said. "It wasn't a year after he left—a year in which I heard of no phone calls or letters, I mind you—that she died. Awful, just awful."

The *Slalom Times* obituary for Lillian Antumbra did not list a cause of death. I could find no one with any information as to any illness Ms. Antumbra may have been suffering from. The hospital staff had no recollection of her seeking treatment for anything, much less anything as highly involved as chemotherapy or anything of that sort. I know, you're thinking HIPAA but you have to speak with a small-town hospital staff like those at Slalom General to understand that these things aren't necessary when "your heart's in the right place."

The obituary said she was survived by her only son, Homer Antumbra, whereabouts unknown. Homer did not attend the funeral. He, in fact, did not know of his mother's death until nearly four months after she was buried.

"He didn't even show up for his momma's funeral," Janice Stewart said, shaking her head with the utmost disapproval only a church lady could muster.

The coroner's report listed Lillian Antumbra's death as "natural causes." Several employees of the coroner's office and hospital—who did not want to be mentioned by name—said there was nothing they could find medically that caused Lily's death. "She just died. No foul play. No pathological reason. Just up and died." I don't think writing "Broken Heart" as a cause of death would have won anybody any favors with their superiors or the state.

Over the course of writing this book, I searched out the Antumbra family seeking interviews, photographs, the whole nine yards, but was turned away at every corner. The general consensus was that they wanted nothing to do with Homer Antumbra, his mother, or my project. That is until I received a phone call from Mary Beth Antumbra, Homer's maternal aunt. She called me up while I was in Nebraska and I scheduled an interview at her place some twenty-five miles outside Slalom in a place called Cool Rock Township.

I'd seen several photos of Lillian Antumbra—all taken at various Slalom Baptist events—and when I met her sister, Mary Beth, I thought the two were nearly spitting images of each other. Both had high and tight ponytails of raven black hair. Both had piercing, dark eyes and high, sharp cheekbones.

Mary Beth Antumbra had several of Homer Antumbra's records sitting out on the coffee table when she led me into her sparsely furnished living room.

"I'm a bit different than my family," she said when I looked up from the records.

"How do you mean?"

"I wish to God we hadn't abandoned them like we did. I wished to God I had been there for Lily and gotten to know Homer," she said.

We hadn't even sat down yet and there were tears in her eyes. Her voice shook with emotion and her face quivered, seeming just barely under her control.

"Would you like some tea?" she asked, turning away and disappearing into the kitchen. I picked up her copy of *blackblackthesky-wasblack* and heard the water running in the other room. The record sleeve was worn from being pulled on and off the shelf. I don't think the emotion was feigned to get into the book (the one in your hands right now). I decided she was genuine.

I crossed the room with the record and put it on her record player, removing the needle from the holder and setting it down gently on the black vinyl. Her speakers crackled to life, then came Homer's gentle picking out of the A minor chord, moving then to the C and back again. By the end of the first verse of "Let It Fall", Mary Beth Antumbra was back in the living room with two steaming cups of Earl Grey.

"Tell me about what happened between Lillian and your family," I said.

"Well, you got to understand where they're coming from first," Mary Beth said. "See, we grew up in the church, almost literally. I remember being there more often than being home."

The Antumbras are centralized in Stetson County, Nebraska, mostly in the Cool Rock Township area. Lillian and Mary Beth's father, George Antumbra, was the preacher at Cool Rock First Baptist, and their mother, Eunice, led the women's group. The family resided in a small trailer behind the church but, according to Mary Beth, spent nearly all their time in the church or the community center a few blocks over from the church.

Along with Mary Beth, Lily also had two brothers, Matthew

and Jacob, both of which followed in the footsteps of their father and went on to become preachers of their own churches; one in Kansas, the other in Oklahoma.

"Daddy about to died when he heard Matt had a band playing in his church. See, the only accompaniment we grew up with was Momma's organ playing. That was all that was allowed. No guitars, no fiddles, no nothing. Just the organ and most times we sung without that. It was saved for special occasions, mostly," Mary Beth said.

"But he came to accept it?"

"Well, I wouldn't say he accepted it. Matt told him that it was a new era for the church and if a little music got the people to fill the pews and hear the Good News then why should he stand in the way?" Mary Beth said. "Daddy never assented to the idea but he eventually stopped harping on it."

"So, what happened between your sister and your family?" I asked again.

"Fox Grayson was coming through Slalom—you know of Fox Grayson and the Disgrace, right?"

I nodded my head.

"See, she [Lily] was just a sophomore and all her little friends were going to that concert and, of course, she wanted to go too," Mary Beth said. "Daddy wouldn't hear of it. He said no and that was that. Lily pushed once or twice but he slapped her and she didn't ask again."

I must've flinched or paled at this simple statement.

"It was his way. He never caused any real pain or injuries. He'd slap us like he was trying to clear our heads and show us that he was the decision maker, and we were the followers." Her smile looked pained.

"Well, Lily was every bit as hardheaded as Daddy. She had it in her brain that she was going to that concert and that was that. She didn't raise no more fuss, didn't fight or buck to get her way like most teenage girls. She just up and snuck out on the night of the concert. We didn't hear her go and probably wouldn't have heard her return if she hadn't been so drunk."

She took a sip from the now cold tea.

"She came in giggling and knocking against every damn thing in the living room. It couldn't have been an hour or so away from sun up either. I tried to get up and out there to her before she could wake up the whole house but I was too late. I had my hand on my bedroom doorknob when I heard Momma and Daddy's door open—it had a squeak to it—and I knew she was toast."

"What happened?" I asked.

Mary Beth Antumbra shook her head and frowned.

"It wasn't pretty. Not at all. I heard him stomp down the hall past my room then quiet. Quiet. I yanked open my door and flew down the hall after him. Lily was sitting on the floor swaying, her arms keeping her up but only just barely. She had this crooked smile on her face like the number seven if it couldn't stand up straight. Daddy was standing above her just staring down. His face didn't show a thing. I tried to get his attention but he acted like he didn't hear me. Lily was giggling and humming snatches of that 'Three Shots' song and completely oblivious to us standing there. The coffee table was crooked, the candles all knocked over. She must've knocked the Bible off it too when she ran into it because it was on the floor over by the couch.

"I said 'Daddy' again but he didn't turn to me. He just stood over Lily until she realized he was there. Then she went rigid for a second in surprise but it caused her to fall over and sent her a-giggling again. I was so scared for her. Daddy said, 'You think this is funny, girl?' And Lily shook her head but she was still smirking. Daddy moved real quick and I flinched thinking he was going to slap her but he picked up the Bible instead. He stood over her, Bible in hand, and tears started coming down Lily's cheeks. She wasn't smiling no more. He didn't say anything. He didn't hit her. He just stood there over her—his back was to me so I couldn't see his face, which I'm kind of glad I couldn't see—then handed down the Bible to her. She took it and looked at it, crying. Daddy turned around and walked past me down the hall, shutting his bedroom door behind him.

"From then on he didn't so much as look at her. It was like she didn't exist. He wouldn't say a word to her. He would talk around her but never directly to her. She finally started getting sick then started showing and it was over. We came home from school one day and all of her stuff was packed into those big trash bags you use for leaves in the fall. It was all sitting outside the trailer and Momma stopped her when she tried coming into the house. Said it wasn't her home no more."

"Jesus," I whispered.

"What could we do?" she snapped. "They [Mr. & Mrs. Antumbra] wouldn't let us so much as speak to her. She stood outside the trailer just a-crying. It was the saddest thing I ever heard. But Momma and Daddy didn't so much as shed a tear. They made us get to our homework like we always had to. Then when we were done they sent us to our rooms to study on the Bible. That was it. I don't remember when she left but come dinner time, Lily wasn't out there anymore, neither were the trash bags. She didn't come to school no more neither."

"Yeah, we just bummed about for a while," Steven Williams said. "We hopped some trains, hitchhiked, walked, the whole hobo thing. That's what we did, yessir."

I spoke with Steven Williams after hearing of him tell stories about traveling with Homer Antumbra (in the years just after his leaving Nebraska) during his concerts and in interviews. Steven Williams is a musician and plays a brand of neo-country and western akin to Roy Acuff but relying more on the Hank Williams (though sharing the same last name, he is of no relation to the late great) and Merle Haggard songbooks. He plays and records as Steven "County Fair" Williams.

"Can you tell me a little more about that?" I asked.

"I mean we were both young men without homes. We just traveled around and drank, mostly. I had this cheap Washburn guitar and taught him some chords after we'd both been drunk for a few days and we took turns playing and singing some old Woody Guthrie songs. It was plumb bum fun, beautiful scenery, shitty scenery, didn't matter. We were smashed and seeing the land," he said, smiling.

In the years following Homer Antumbra's death, Steven "County Fair" Williams has joined in the legal circus that has surrounded the royalty battle involving a handful of people (of which I'll address in a later chapter. I mention it here to give the reader the opportunity to cast a wary eye upon the words of Steven Williams as they may be skewed or embellished with the legal proceedings pending).

"We were all over the place. Detroit, Minneapolis, Indianapolis, Louisville, Nashville, Biloxi, New Orleans, Kansas City, you name it. The more we traveled, the more our focus shifted towards the guitar and the songs. From those Woody Guthrie songs I taught him, Ant started strumming and playing songs of his own. He always had a notebook on him and he wrote lyrics all the time. Then he'd sit with the guitar and try to put the two on the same page."

"How long were you two traveling mates?"

"It must've been a year or so. It's hard to tell exactly when you're drunk all the time," County Fair said and grinned his hyena grin again.

"He disappeared a few times too," Williams said. "One time with *my* guitar and I would've sworn to you then—in my drunken state—that I would've killed the bastard had I found him. Turns out, he went back to Nebraska to bury his momma. He showed up a few weeks afterwards, I think it was in Minneapolis, and handed me back my guitar. He had a few dollars and went out and got one of his own then."

"What happened next?" I asked.

"Well, he started playing the songs he wrote and the ones I taught him and got some gigs around the clubs there in Minneapolis and stuck around. I kept on bummin' 'round."

Homer Antumbra got his first real start in the world of music in the Twin Cities, mostly in the seedier sections on the outskirts of Minneapolis. He took his Fender dreadnought from bar to bar, playing for a few dollars from the club and the few from the patrons, and often just for drinks. Seems he resurfaced after his mother's death in the North with a guitar and a drinking problem.

"He used to come out to the club a lot—most of the time already drunk—with his guitar and get up on the stage and play these weird, sad songs," Joey Malone said. "I never cared much for them but he could also play some old-time songs that a lot of people really liked and I let him play because of those."

Joey Malone is the owner and operator of Joey's Place, a bar with a small stage next to the bathrooms, out in industrial Minneapolis. I spoke to him at his bar over a pitcher of beer.

"What can you tell me about Homer Antumbra from those days?" I asked.

"He was a drunk. A sloppy, pitiful drunk. He could play that guitar and sing though."

Joey Malone said 'drunk' like it was something absolutely profane, which seemed odd for the proprietor of a drinking establishment.

"No homo but he had a beautiful voice," he said. "It would shut everybody up when he started singing those weird, slow songs of his. He could stop a crowd with his voice. It was weird. I didn't like it. The louder the place is the more drinks are being ordered, but I wouldn't let him play more than a few of those songs before

I'd kick him out or have him play something more upbeat."

"Do you remember any of those songs? The words maybe?"

He shook his head and sipped from his dirty glass.

"Nope. There were a lot of songs about animals and people and the *dark*. Like it was something that could reach out and get you," he said then laughed. "Like a kid's dream, nightmare I mean. You know, afraid of the dark or something.

"I tried to book him on a regular basis. We were in a bit of a drought, talent-wise, at that time. The bands were playing at other places and I had to keep something happening to keep people coming through the doors. I'd set up several shows for him but he would fuck it up. He'd show up for one and be absolutely amazing. You couldn't help but watch him, it was that damn voice. Then, he'd miss the next two or show up too shitfaced to talk but he could still play but it wasn't pretty. Other times he'd show up drunk but not too drunk, you know? And the show would be okay. Just okay," he said.

He refilled the empty pitcher and sat back down with it at the bar.

"He was unpredictable. A *drunk*," he said.

This time 'drunk' served as the explanation for 'unpredictable'.

I had barely finished my first glass of beer when he refilled the pitcher. I don't know how he drank most of it because he was doing all the talking.

"So, I worked out a system, a deal, you could say," Mr. Malone said. "I'd let him play whenever he showed up but he couldn't be too drunk already. Then I wouldn't pay him. I'd let him play for drinks. This guaranteed me at least forty minutes to an hour of solid entertainment before he started getting sloppy. Then I'd kick him off the stage and send him out the door."

It appears this went on for some months. Homer Antumbra actually developed somewhat of a following, word got around about a captivating performer playing at Joey's Place, and new faces showed up in hopes of seeing him. Cliff Branger and Dave Ingles were two such new faces.

"We went out there together—we were together then—to see this character, this Homer Antumbra," Cliff Branger said. "At first we heard his name was Antibra, which we thought was hilarious. It was after seeing him play again and talking to him afterwards that we learned his real name."

Cliff Branger is the owner of a small music venue and bar nearer to downtown Minneapolis. His partner at the time, Dave Ingles, owns a record store not three blocks from Branger's club. They regularly went out in search of developing artists to book at Branger's club. It was their thing.

"I can't remember how we heard about him. We just had our ears to the streets, I guess. We heard just about everything that went on musically in the Cities. Anyway, we went down to Joey's Place—which is absolutely disgusting, by the way—and watched him play."

"Actually, we went down there a few times before we actually caught a set," Dave Ingles said. "See, he [Antumbra] wasn't exactly showing up on a regular basis and we ended up spending a few hours at that dingy place, Cliff going blotto as per usual, and me smoking cigarette after cigarette."

The two are no longer romantically involved and would not agree to a joint interview. I spoke with Cliff Branger first, at his club, then Dave Ingles, at his record store.

"When we finally got to see him," Cliff Branger said, "he just blew us away. He stood up there, swaying a bit from the alcohol, and played these midnight folk operas. They were like dispatches from some other world, akin to ours but just outside the normal person's range of perception."

"Do you remember the songs?"

"They didn't make it to any album. I'm not sure if they even made it down complete in one form to his notebook—he always had a notebook somewhere near at hand. We've—I mean—*I* have heard him play a song dozens of ways, the lyrics changing, the story changing, the chords or key changing. He was still learning and we—*I*—got to see the transformation firsthand. It was special."

"We went out and saw him together a handful of times and each time he was good," Dave Ingles said. "Sometimes he was crazy good but then others he would be hammered and just good. He was like that. Anyway, Cliff booked him at his place, after I prodded him to do so for days on end, and I gave him a job at the store [Ingles' New & Used Records]."

"How was he as an employee?"

"He was a very hard worker. I think it was his first steady job or something. He was deathly serious about it and never showed up drunk and never drank much while he was working. Working at the store, there tends to be a lot of downtime. In that time, I introduced him to a lot of music he hadn't heard before. I'd go out and pick up a record from the bins and drop the needle on it and, if it was something I knew something about, I'd tell him about it. *Blood on the Tracks*, *Black Sabbath*, Prine's *Sweet Revenge*, you name it. Anything and everything. Bowie, Marley, Van Morrison, Rod Stewart, Tom Petty, Little Richard, whatever the mood called for." Dave Ingles smiled and went on. "It got to be that he'd get there before me—he might have slept there a few times but I'm not sure—and already have the speakers blasting something. He became the master of the stereo and played whatever caught his ear."

"You know, I don't think he would've got the experience he got from us—me—anywhere else. No chance in Hell if he hadn't gotten out of Nebraska. Can you imagine a middle-aged gay couple befriending a young musician in rural Nebraska?" Cliff Branger said then laughed. "It just wouldn't happen. Better chance of seeing a unicorn or finding Bigfoot."

"The stuff he was working on sounded old and new at the same time," Cliff Branger said. "He'd use regular old chords—F, G, D, Am, C—but coupled with his voice and the words it became something eerie. Timeless, almost. Other people playing would be singing, 'My heart aches, my liver's bad, I just want to be held so bad' or something as heavy handed. Homer stood up there, at first alone—just him and the guitar—and tell these spooky stories of being followed or chasing something that is never quite explicitly defined."

Though their breakup was bitter, both Branger and Ingles had nothing but kind words and stories regarding Homer Antumbra. They let him sleep over at their places, ride the couch until he could get a place of his own, and helped him get a new, better guitar and, eventually, a four-track recorder. He stayed put in the Twin Cities for almost a year, working, writing, performing. It was there he first began his love affair with the recording process, which lasted until his reason left him. He also got his first start playing in a band there.

"Ant was unpredictable," Keith Skees said. "He'd show up sober and closed off or drunk and open to experimenting with sounds and different tunings and instruments. Sometimes, he wouldn't show up at all. We'd be booked to play some shows—not just at Cliff's Place—and he'd show up in a dark mood and decide that he didn't want us to play with him that night. That the Truth called for *just* him at that moment. No accompaniment.

"Sure it pissed us off. Pissed me off more than anyone, I'd say. I loved to play. That's what I was there for. Why the Hell would I show up with a drum set if I wasn't going to get a chance to play it?

Why wouldn't you just pick up a phone and call me? Let me know that 'the Truth' wouldn't be needing me that night. Why waste my time?"

There were several other musicians that played with Homer Antumbra during this time frame with similar stories.

"I got him some gigs at some other places around the Cities, at first," Cliff Branger said. "But it didn't take him long to develop his own drawing power. People would come to him and have him open for some pretty big time touring acts or to headline a weekend night at some of the smaller places."

Several concert flyers from this time period have survived and show that Homer Antumbra opened for the likes of the Stereochews, Shoebox, Flaccid Warmer, Birchwood Mamas, Inkblot Boys, and more.

"He started bands, musicians gravitated to him," Branger said. "What he was doing looked, from the outside, so simple yet anybody with any iota of musical inkling could tell it was sorcery. It was not something that could be imitated or learned."

"Man, Ant was a genius," longtime bandmate Brandon Fulkers said. "I'm not just saying that because you drove all the way out here to talk to me about him. I seriously, genuinely believe that and am not afraid to say it. Sure, he got a few people bent all out of shape but that is the way with geniuses. He could bring more from whoever he was playing with than even they thought was there. I'm proof.

"Now, I've been playing since I could talk. Music is and has always been my life. But I have my limits just like the next guy. Nobody is limitless. Nobody except maybe Ant.

"We'd get together twice, sometimes three times a week for practice and he'd always have some new idea for a song or a way to rework something we'd already been playing to get a fresh spin.

He'd play what he had and the thoughts just struck you like lightning bolts. I'd hear him play something new, some three or four or maybe just two chords and a line, and the concept would miraculously be there in my head. Like a coffee percolator. He'd play what he had and it was like he knew you already had your part there and he just boiled it to the top, made the coffee. We'd play it a few times and that was like adding a bit of cream and sugar until you got it just the way you like it, just the way it was supposed to be. And it always went like that. Always."

Homer Antumbra played with a throng of musicians during this time, Brandon Fulkers being the only one from the Twin Cities that stuck with him, made the cut. He played on nearly every album Homer Antumbra recorded in which there were accompanying musicians.

> *The haze of the path comes from the freezing of the Way.*
> *There are places, people I knew, that are dead.*
> *Ways of living, closed to me, also dead.*
> *Becoming what I must, not what I promised never to be.*
> —From the notebooks of Homer Antumbra

Chapter Five
Find the Light, Walk the Way, Fight the Darkness

"He was always reading too," Cliff Branger said. "I'd see him with *The Art of War* one week, Ernest Hemingway the next, then *Anna Karenina* the next. He was everywhere with his musical interests too, at least at first. I'd walk into Dave's store that morning to hear Bob Dylan, bring them lunch from Pascal's and there'd be Tom Waits coming through the speakers. I'd come over to walk them back to the bar after the store closed and hear Copland. He was searching, surveying. The world was a big place, suffocatingly full of ideas and he was trying to find some sense of meaning in it all."

"We weren't religious then," Dave Ingles said. "I'm still not, but one day at the store Homer said he was planning on going over to the Baptist church on 31st Street. It was a Wednesday and he was supposed to play at Cliff's that night. When I mentioned this, he just looked up at me from the bin he was alphabetizing and said, 'There are some things that I just have to do.' That was that. I went to the back office and called up Cliff and told him that Homer wouldn't be playing that night and for him not to push it because

A.S. Coomer

Homer said he had to go to church.

"He'd never been to church as far as we knew then. He'd never made it a point to go, that we could tell. Sunday mornings were for hangovers, you know? He was always nursing one to one degree or another. So when he said he was going to church that Wednesday night I figured he was needing some help or guidance or something."

"Did he start attending regularly?" I asked.

"No. He only went that one time as far as I know. I think it was more of a spiritual searching thing. Like he was always reading and listening to something new, searching for the right words or sounds. Trying to find something that fit his scheme of things. It was like he was surveying everything that claimed to 'know.' Trying on different clothes, looking for the right fit."

> *The Way has shed light.*
> *Another Darkness enfolds.*
> *The night snow hardens.*
> —From the notebooks of Homer Antumbra

The notebooks of Homer Antumbra from this time period are full of little haikus (like the one quoted above) as well as tankas. He was experimenting more and more with highly structured and stylized poetry both in his notebooks and his songwriting.

His poetry and lyrics were focused on searching. Songs about seekers in the night, though it's never explicitly stated what exactly was sought, just 'the Way,' 'the Path,' and, finally, 'the Light'. There are loads of interviewers, reviewers, and critics misconstruing this notion—seeking the Light—as being a thinly veiled reference to Christianity, to seek God's Light, Jesus's Light, etc. I think this is too simplistic and downright erroneous.

"They're all religious songs," he said.

Yes, but religion to Homer Antumbra was not a closely connected series of rules or guidelines but a manner of living. It was the constant search for perfection. The desire to be honest, always in the moment, true. The age-old idea of a force of Good forever being embattled with the force of Evil precedes Christianity or any other such present-day religion. It is as old as man, as thought. As is the pursuit of a sense of purpose. Homer Antumbra's religion was the combined plight for answers, or at least the semblance of answers, to these questions.

"He was always writing these weird, metaphysical dribbles on finding the way," Keith Skees said. "I think he thought he was a goddamn Buddhist monk or something. I'd try to get him to play something that would get the place rocking, you know, something like *Like a Rolling Stone*, or *Can't Get No Satisfaction* [sic], but he never would go for it. [Antumbra] said those songs were good but playing them wouldn't be telling the Truth. Like the damn T was capitalized when he'd say it."

"Sometimes I'd forget what we were doing and just listen to the lyrics," Brandon Fulkers said. "Especially those first days. He was singing these soul-searching poems and I just couldn't wrap my head around some of them and couldn't get enough of them. I'd end up playing something so simplistic that afterwards, especially after cutting it for the first time, I'd get embarrassed. Thought people heard, and if they were listening to anything other than Homer's bits, they'd think I was a hack or something. I'd have to really focus on what I was doing, especially the first few times I heard a new song."

"We had to bail him out of jail a few times," Cliff Branger said. "He'd get picked up at the railroad yards or some such crazy place and be drunk. He never tried to start a fight or hurt anybody or steal anything but drinking was something he did alone. Like it was some battle he had to take part in, wrestling with inner demons, you know, that sort of thing.

"I'd never lecture him after we'd bail him out. That was Dave's thing. I just helped him to the couch and covered him with a blanket and let him be. That's the best way, I think. Set out a big glass of water and just let it be. Things, especially really personal things, have to be worked out on a really personal level. Moralizing isn't going to do anything other than give somebody a preacherman phobia."

"Cliff said you all had to bail Homer out of jail on a few occasions," I said.

Dave Ingles nodded his head but looked annoyed.

"He would tell you that," he said.

"I'm trying to get the whole picture, Mr. Ingles. Not just the good stuff."

"Dave. It's Dave. I know. It's just weird saying stuff about things like that after a man's dead. He can't defend himself, you know?"

I nodded and waited.

"I remember one time we got the call. It was something like four in the morning and piss pouring rain. We go down to the station and this cop—the *arresting officer*—he pulls us aside, makes sure we're close to Homer, like real friends, then tells us that he was wondering whether or not we wanted to have him committed, a 72-hour hold," Dave Ingles said. "Of course we asked him why on earth he thought something like that was necessary."

"What did he say?"

"He said that when they picked Homer up he was shirtless, drunk and raving about not being able to find the light. The cop said that he was standing under a streetlight over in the warehouse district and staring up at the light that wasn't working. He was crying, hysterical."

It was under the darkened, bulbous night sky, rain belching down onto the dirty streets around me that I saw the Light. I looked up and saw it shining down. I opened my mouth to cheer and dropped the bottle. It shattered. When I looked back up the Light had gone out. I felt so alone. It was there. I had seen it. Finally. Then it was gone. I looked away and it had fled. Fled from me. Receded back into the Darkness. I tore at my clothes feeling suffocated then the flashing blue lights came and I was taken away.

—From the notebooks of Homer Antumbra

"When he woke up that next afternoon, he looked like a steaming turd sandwich," Cliff Branger said. "I mean he was hung-the-fuck-over. That being said, he had this little smile on his face and when he wasn't puking his guts out or under three feet of covers, he'd be scribbling in his notebook. When he passed back out I read what he wrote—feeling every bit the prying parent, the diary reading daddy—it was about seeing the Light and it leaving. I pictured him standing out there, shirtless in the rain looking for his true sense of self or salvation or whatever and I felt like scooping the guy up and just holding him. It was so sad."

It wasn't sad to Homer Antumbra. This drunken episode, including his arrest, was the germination of a lifelong pursuit of the Light. In his haze, Homer had seen the Light and it was more than just an ordinary, run of the mill, malfunctioning streetlight; it was the Way. He saw the Path lined up before him and after the alcohol washed out of his system, he saw the moment for what it was: Illumination.

Filled with rocks,
Can't hold my head up,

A.S. Coomer

"The other times were just drunken arrests, nothing out of the ordinary," Dave Ingles said. "I'm pretty used to them from bailing Cliff out over and over again. But after that night when the cop wanted to put him in the looney bin, Homer changed. He was more focused than he had ever been. He started the process of solidifying the lineup of the band he'd been assembling and booked some studio time at Studio Eh downtown."

"What do you mean he changed?"

"He was driven. Before he'd been mostly looking. It was like he'd figured it out, had decided, made a decision about something. It's hard to describe. The songs changed too. He had a whole slew of these searching songs but the ones he wrote from that night on were mostly personified or in the third person. It wasn't 'I'm searching' anymore. There were characters—always characters, most of the time nameless—that served as starting and ending points for the continuous search for meaning in life.

"But God, it's too easy to break these things down. It's way more complicated than that. Life is so much more than just a few words uttered by a sad man in the waning light of the afternoon."

I told him that line was definitely making the book and we laughed.

"He woke up a goddamn prophet, I swear," Cliff Branger said. "He was all: the Way, the Path, the Light, Shining a Light, Fight the Darkness. It was a bit much at first but you could tell he was serious, deathly serious. And the more you listened to the words of the songs, the more you could peel a layer or two away and find it still added up, still made sense in some weird, hard to explain, mystical sort of way. It was heavy. I still can't listen to Homer's music on a regular basis, it's too heavy."

The song structure for Homer Antumbra's music during this period widely varied, as it would over the course of his career. There were songs that clocked in at less than a minute; short, intense tone poems reflecting on the Light or the Darkness or the struggle between the two. A critique of Homer's first album snubbed it for its lack of personal lyric but how much more personal can it get than struggling to be Good in a world of Evil? How much more sincere could it get than pouring your heart out on tracks such as "Feeble" when he sings:

> *I've made the flame*
> *I'll shine my feeble light*
> *Waving it towards the shadows*
> *In the dark and windy night.*
> *May this be enough,*
> *For the breadth of momentary illumination,*
> *However brief,*
> *May this be enough.*

Chapter Six

R e c o r d i n g ,   M a k i n g   R e c o r d s ,
T e l l i n g   t h e   T r u t h

Homer Antumbra quickly grew in status and competency. The four-track recorder became an excellent tool for honing the sound of a song but he wanted to get into the studio and make an album. Something produced, more polished than his home demos: a quality sound recording.

"Cliff likes to say it was him that started pushing Homer to record but that simply isn't the truth," Dave Ingles said. "Homer was working his way towards the studio ever since he started writing the songs. Seeing whatever he saw that night we had to go bail him out was the tipping point. He'd been at the cusp."

"*blackblacktheskywasblack* was a revelation," Brandon Fulkers said. "Homer came out to my place and said he had booked three days to record at Studio Eh and that we needed to have a few run throughs of the songs. I called up Brian [Phillips] and Jacob [Slither] and Keith [Skees] and got them to come over and we went through the twelve songs Homer wanted to record. Those practice sessions were tense. Homer was intense and Brian and Jacob had their own ideas for the songs but Homer wasn't having any of it.

"It's so weird how some people just don't fit together. I mean, when Homer and I'd play, it worked. It was like the puzzle pieces lined up and, of course, it had to make a picture of something. But with Brian and Jacob it wasn't like that at all. To Homer it was all about the songs. Guys like Brian and Jacob came and went in droves because they wanted it to be about their playing this riff over that or the technical aspects of their solo or bridge work. They came and went because they didn't fit. The band was there to provide the songs with the proper atmosphere, not to overshadow the thing. They just didn't get it and that's why they didn't make the record."

The band that ended up going into the studio consisted of Homer Antumbra on guitar, harmonica and vocals, Brandon Fulkers on lead and slide guitars, and a veteran of the Minneapolis music scene, Janice Angela Steinbeck, on standup bass.

Janice Angela Steinbeck, like Fulkers, would be with Homer Antumbra for the vast majority of his career. They met after one of Homer's sets at Cliff's Place. Steinbeck, a hard-drinking woman at that time—known around the scene as 'Drunken Angel' or 'Steiner'—came up to Homer praising the songs and the two went out on a night of drinking together that culminated in Steinbeck quitting her current band, The Spit City Charmers, and joining Homer's.

"Man, he was up there just *playing*," Janice Steinbeck said. "Playing from somewhere I'd never been fully. I mean, we all have our darknesses, I've been down in the valley most of my life, but here was this guy up there singing about it. He'd come back. Been there and come back with a story to tell. I wanted nothing more than to be a part of that."

"I heard you all hung out after you saw him for the first time. What all did y'all do?" I asked.

"We never fucked, if that's what you're asking."

My face flushed and I stammered out that that's not what I was implying and she laughed.

"Jesus, you're uptight. Yeah, we went out drinking. Picked up a bottle and just went street walking. Talking."

"What kinds of things did you talk about?"

"Music. Life. The stars. Cliff and Dave. The Cities. Everything. Anything that popped up in our minds. It was always like that between Ant and me. We felt like soul siblings, on the same wavelength. I told him I wanted to make music with him then quit my band."

The plan was to have Keith Skees on drums but after the botched prep sessions for the album, Antumbra and Skees parted ways. The album was recorded largely without drums, relying mostly on Steinbeck's bass for time, but Studio Eh's owner and operator, Jamie Kurtz, sat behind the kit and filled in on drums for three of the album's eight tracks.

"Homer Antumbra was a machine," Jamie Kurtz said. "Those first few records I did with him, he'd come in with the bare bones of a song, usually his part nearly complete, and lay it out for the rest of the band. Then they'd record it within the first three takes after rehearsing it maybe once or twice. He didn't give anyone time to overthink anything. It was 'Here it is, figure out your part and let's get it down.' There was no wasted time or effort. Very efficient, machine-like. The songs were mostly personal then. Some cryptic lines from the underside of his soul and an equally stark set of chords or notes. All I had to do was hit record and help flesh out the sound, which was almost equal parts of heavy silence."

"You played drums on several of those songs, didn't you?"

"Yeah. Nothing special. Just enough to fill in the gap the songs left for the drums. It was like that. Each person was there to contribute to the songs. You weren't in a band, per se. You were help-ing craft this piece of art that would forever be accessible once we recorded it. It was special."

While Homer Antumbra was recording *blackblacktheskywasblack*, buzz around his live performance as well as the studio sessions was getting around.

"I hadn't seen him yet," Herschell 'Hershey' Walters said. "I'd heard about him and the songs he was writing and playing. They were supposed to be this intense, heavy, dark thing; *an experience* somebody told me. An experience. I heard that and I thought, man, I *have* to be a part of that."

Herschell Walters, better known as Hershey, was a stalwart of the Northern Alternative, as the music scene for the region was known then. His record label, Glow-In-The-Dark-Skeleton Records, had been the watershed of the scene, releasing such pivotal albums as DiseasedChildren's *Here It Comes*, all of Ronald Wheelwright's recordings, and most of Spandex Foxtrot's better albums. He had his nose or hands in just about everything in the area, especially in the Twin Cities where the label's office was located.

"I went out and saw him and his band play," he said. "It was just before they were going into Studio Eh to record the songs that would become *black* [sic]. I was blown away. They were up there playing and they were right. It felt right. It really did feel like the Truth, as Ant always said he was telling. And the show did feel like an experience. It was powerful."

Hershey Walters spoke with Homer and the band after their show that night at Cliff's Place and found out they were to go into the studio the next day. Being a personal friend and having released several of the recordings that came out of Studio Eh, Walters called his friend Jamie Kurtz and asked him to keep him updated on the band's recording sessions. During the three days the band recorded, Kurtz called up Walters after the band had finished for the night and had him come to the studio to listen to the rough mixes.

"I can't even describe it fully," Walters said. "When I heard those recordings it was a moment of clarity. I knew this was the reason I had started the label. This man's songs, the band's music, was what needed to be on the label, if nothing else."

Walters signed Homer Antumbra just two days after he and the band had finished tracking their first album.

The album was finished, the rough mixes, at least, in those three days and was mixed and mastered within the next week and a half. Homer Antumbra met with Hershey Walters on a nearly nightly basis, prepping the album for release including extended discussions about the packaging, artwork, liner notes, etc.

The album was released not three months later. This is crazy fast when you stop and think about it. Sure, any kid with GarageBand can record a collection of songs and release it digitally on a single day but the zeal of the label and band to get a professional, intrinsically detailed hard copy release done in three months is something to marvel at.

blackblacktheskywasblack was released both as an LP and as a CD. It features a haunting oil painting from surrealist Stanley McKinley depicting a barren, lonely highway crossroads. It looks like it could've come directly out of Homer Antumbra's poem *Nightcrawler*. Staring at the beautiful piece you come to almost expect Robert Johnson, guitar over his slender shoulder, to step into the scene to meet the hoof-footed Devil himself.

The album quickly sold out and it was decided that Homer Antumbra and his band should tour to support the CD version while the next order of vinyl was being pressed. Homer Antumbra had been planted firmly in Minneapolis for nearly a year. His diary reflects his desire to "chase the horizon" and "keep my feet moving."

Homer and the band embarked on a three-week tour that took them down the Midwest all the way to New Orleans then over to and up the east coast all the way to Charlotte, North Carolina, before returning home to play the second pressing's record release show at Cliff's Place.

PART TWO

HUNTING AND HUNTED AND HAUNTED / BATTLING THE DARK & SHINING THE LIGHT

Chapter Seven

Touring: Troubles & Triumphs

*It's hard telling the Truth sometimes. Standing there in
the face of it, the firing line, it's easier to just turn away
or say anything else. It's easier sometimes to run away.
Most times really.*
—From the notebooks of Homer Antumbra

The tour had a run of usually three or four nights working in a row
then a day or two off, mostly to cover the vast distances between
cities. Walters secured a 15-person passenger van formerly owned
and operated by a local church for the band, in which they traveled,
slept most nights and hauled all of their equipment. The van still
displayed the name (Twin Cities' First United Methodist) and
phone number of the church on its driver's side and rear door.

"I can't tell you how many angry phone calls I got from that
damn church," Hershey Walters laughs. "Jimmy Ross, that's the
guy from the church who sold me the thing, would call screaming,
'Get our name and number off that van immediately. I just got a
phone call saying some half-dressed woman stumbled out of the van
on the side of the road in Alabama and threw up all over herself.'"

That was not the only call he received regarding the van and its occupants.

"This other time, it was a Monday morning, Jimmy Ross called me again and was downright furious. He said, 'What in God's name is going on with that van? This time some little old lady in Charlottesville, North Carolina called to tell me that it was disrespectful to litter from a church vehicle. She said that a steady stream of empty beer cans and bottles were flying from the van's open windows on the highway.' At this point, I was sick of the motherfucker calling me all the time. I told him that the vehicle had been stolen at gunpoint and the police told me the guy who took it was a serial rapist of boys."

The first tour had critics hailing the band and its debut album. *The Kansas City Star* hailed both the live show and the album as "Triumphant, emotional twisting, and shapeshifting." After the band's New Orleans gig, *The Times-Picayune* wrote that, "No shortcuts [were] taken, every nuance and ounce of energy on the record is there in the live show. There and then some."

Sales of *blackblacktheskywasblack* were greatly exceeding anything Glow-In-The-Dark-Skeleton Records had ever released. Walters found himself struggling to keep the thing in print. He'd send another order for both the vinyl and CD to the plant as it sold out and by the time he got the order he'd already have sold more than he'd had pressed.

"I had to get them back into the studio," Walters said. "The demand was outrageous. That album was hotter than Hell. I couldn't believe it. Well, on one hand I could but on the other, I figured, Bob Dylan's first album—though incredible—was a flop and I, sort of, expected something of the same. I mean, I knew the songs were great and the recording was primo but . . . you just never expect something like that to happen, you know?"

Tour life is an interesting thing. There are extended periods of idleness despite the constant flow of passing scenery from the van's windows. Veterans of the touring life, like Janice Angela Steinbeck, were used to it, used to being able to both interact with the bandmates around them and to retreat into one's self when necessary. Also, there was alcohol. Lots of alcohol.

"Drunken Angel lived up to her name," Brandon Fulkers said. "I mean, she went to bed with the bottle in her hand and first thing she did when she woke up was take a swig. I mean, before she even yawned that girl was taking swallows of Jim Beam. But she was never sloppy or out of control. I don't know how she did it. I mean, if I had the quantity she had, I'd of pissed myself and not been able to get out of the van."

"Yeah, I used to drink a little bit then," Janice Angela Steinbeck said. "Homer and I both did. I think I had him beat though. At least, I could function a hell of a lot better than he could when I'd been at it."

There are no reports of interrupted shows on this tour, like there would be on tours in the not too distant future and the mishaps of the immediate past. There are no reviews of the shows, either online or in print (that I could find), of Homer Antumbra being drunk on stage. There are no reports of him forgetting lyrics, falling over, slurring his words (few though they were between songs), or anything of the sort. It seems that, for that time period at least, he was on the somewhat straight and narrow.

"Sure he was drinking," Brandon Fulkers said. "We all were. But he was fine. I mean, it didn't seem like he had a problem or anything. Not any more than I had a problem."

The band picked up multi-instrumentalist Skip Lewis for the tour.

A.S. Coomer

He covered drums, mostly brushes on the snare and hi-hat, as well as organ, steel guitar and viola.

"He'd always be working on something," Lewis said. "Writing songs, poems, stories, or reading some incomprehensibly thick book. Ant was some sort of machine that would fall apart if he didn't have a project or something happening, something to keep his hands and mind busy."

"I don't remember where we were when he got the call from Hershey about making another record. Louisiana or somewheres. He'd been playing a lot of Woody Guthrie in the van and decided that we should do an EP of old-time covers, something akin to *Dust Bowl Ballads*. Hershey was all for it. That first album was selling like hotcakes and he needed to get something else in print while the gettin' was good."

Stage fright is a very common thing, even to tenured performers such as Bob Dylan. It seems that no matter how many times you perform it still remains to some degree or another, oftentimes changing with the personal circumstances of the performer as well as the circumstances surrounding shows. Homer Antumbra had stage fright. This, of course, is not an earth-shattering fact as it's common knowledge the artist also had severe social anxiety and was deeply introspective.

"He'd take off his glasses when we played every night," Steinbeck said. "He didn't, or couldn't—I'm not sure which—stand to look out at the crowd when we were playing. His vision was shit too, so I'm sure it was just a wash of color and faceless people standing out there below us."

"He had a way of leaning in close and staring down hard," Lewis said. "Not squinting or straining like to see but just looking at ya hard. Seeing into you. It was unnerving."

This, of course, was when Homer Antumbra had his glasses off.

"We'd be playing and he'd want to try something—he did that a lot, just say 'let's try this' and start playing some song we'd never heard that he probably was writing right there on the spot—and after we'd given it a go, he'd come over to discuss a part or something and, I swear to God, it was like he was looking into my damn soul. Those eyes were hard and piercing."

The faces swim in a blur. Smears of color sometimes dotted with the dim lights dull reflection like starred pinpricks from where their eyes should be. Sometimes the yawning darkness and glistening whites of gaping mouths, flashing like the opening and closing of tectonic plates. It'd been easier this way at first, when we'd just started out [on the blackblacktheskywasblack tour] and still worried about putting on a good show, whatever weight that actually holds.

—From the notebooks of Homer Antumbra

"He'd take off these battered glasses and drop them in the Gibson's case then turn to the mic and start the sets," Steinbeck said.

Standing there in light, if the place had stage lights (or a stage for that matter) and staring out at a live-action impressionistic depiction of a barroom: moving, smoking, drinking, laughing, cussing, clapping, scowling, faceless smudges of color. I'd slow my breathing then play the songs. Move the fingers into the shapes. Weave the words into the pictures, the stories, the Truth. It'd been easier not seeing their faces, easier just seeing the collection. Now they all looked like that, faceless half-beings, shapes darting in the light and shadows, with the glasses or not. It's not easy now though. Not in the slightest.

—From the notebooks of Homer Antumbra

The man took to the stage like it was his final hearing.
He had the guitar already strapped across his shoulder
and walked briskly across to the microphone. He ripped
his glasses from his face as the stage lights brightened,
dropping them onto his Marshall amplifier. He turned
back to the crowd and his fingers were already working,
shaping and picking the first notes of the first song of the
most intense and draining live performance I have ever
witnessed.

From *The Set-Up/Breakdown Magazine*

"We were just getting to know each other musically," Janice Angel Steinbeck said. "We were learning what we did together, you know? How to talk. Music in a band is a conversation between the members. Shooting the shit and telling stories with notes and all that. We'd just wait for him to kick things off and followed his lead. It was so nerve-racking during the first few moments of the shows during that first tour. We just didn't have the miles together to make it comfortable. Strangers on a first date, you know? That said, as soon as Ant would start it was like the road opened up, like he was a snowplow clearing the way. He'd start and I knew exactly where I should be, what I should do, how it was going to be. It was . . . so many things for me."

At the end of the tour, Skip Lewis found he was more and more often sitting behind the drum kit. This left a bit of a hole in the at-mospherics of the songs as he couldn't provide any organ or steel guitar or lead licks if he was stuck keeping time. As any musician will attest, songs change as they move through time; the more they're played the more is infused. Tones change, words change, directions change. The songs the band was playing during that first string of road dates were of no exception to this rule. The songs stretched, breathed, matured. The timing slowed and steadied, requiring the drums, and the sound became more experimental, probing.

"When we got back to the Cities, we had a meeting with Hershey and decided we needed a drummer," Brandon Fulkers said. "Don't get me wrong, Skip is more than competent behind the kit but his other skills—organ, slide-guitar—were of more value to the songs. Between me, Angel, Skip and Homer, we'd played with nearly every damn drummer in the Twin Cities. None were a good fit, either stylistically or esoterically."

A recent grad school dropout, fleeing the scripted life already put in place for him, had entered the scene while the band was on the road. Stephen Michael Harold Jr. fled from the University of Minnesota where he was midway through a master's program in economics. His father was the financial baron, Stephen Michael Harold Sr., of Harold Advisors, and his mother, Shirley, was a well-known socialite and philanthropist.

"Man, I just ran," Stephen Michael Harold Jr. said. "I didn't take anything with me either, really. Toothbrush and some clothes and the drums. I just left all my shit in my apartment and went out and got a cheap room above Cliff's Place. Started playing drums in some cock-rock band and smoking pot. I didn't want to manage anyone's money, that didn't feel like me at all."

When the band returned from the tour, Hershey had already scoped out the new talent and took the band out to see him play with the 'cock-rock band' he was with. After the performance, they bought him some drinks and lured him away from the lucrative spot with the band he was playing with, preying on his artistic leanings.

A.S. Coomer

"Hershey and Homer came up," Harold said. "I think Angel and Skip were somewhere at the bar too. They bought a pitcher of this really dark, potent beer and sat me in a booth. I guess I'm a pretty easy book to read or something. I mean look at me . . ." Harold opened his arms, presenting himself: a short, wiry, bushy haired, bespectacled, sensitive-looking young man. "Hershey did all the talking. Homer just sat there and stared. It was rather unnerving, really. He said things like, 'We both know this isn't your gig.' And 'You're not made to play for the frat jerks and dumb blondes.' He said that Homer Antumbra and his band were looking for a drummer, a competent one with an understanding of the subtle nuances of artistic merit, then slipped me a copy *blackblacktheskywasblack*.

"I went home that night and listened to the thing, start to finish, like ten times in a row. Just sat there sitting cross-legged on the shitty carpet of my shitty studio apartment in front of the speakers. Somebody—previous tenant, I guess—had left this monstrous and ancient stereo there. I couldn't pick up the CD's booklet. I couldn't move. I couldn't do anything but listen. It was so beautiful and so sad and so everything I felt at the time. I called up Hershey, it must've been four in the morning or some shit by that time, and told him that I was in."

Stephen Michael Harold Jr., whom his bandmates—minus Homer Antumbra—referred to as Mikey or Specs, didn't get to play the CD reissue show at Cliff's Place but was in attendance of the performance.

"I don't know which I was more blown away with: the recording or the live performance. They were both equally—though very different from each other—impressive, innovating and captivating. The songs from the album were fresh in mind after having played nothing else for the past twenty-four hours and when I saw them play them live I was shocked to find them changed. At first, I had that familiar feeling of being cheated by the performer. You know when you grow up with a record and finally get to see the artist or band or whatever and they don't play the songs exactly like they recorded them. But after the first three songs I couldn't feel that way anymore. I just couldn't.

"The songs had morphed into what they were meant to be at that moment. When they were recorded that's what they were. Then, when the band got up on that little stage at Cliff's [Place] they played the only form the songs were in at that time. The only form they could be. It was beautiful. I was riveted and excited for the first time in my life. I was going to be a part of that. I watched Skip behind the drums and knew that the songs would change again once I was back there and he was taking over the organ or slide or whatever. I was ecstatic."

The band took up practicing and working on the songs they would go into Studio Eh with in just two short weeks to record. The EP, composed entirely of cover songs, was initially titled *oldlikenew* but, upon its release, was dubbed *thesesongsiforgot*. Three of the five songs came from a series of recordings from FSA camps in California from the 1940s that Homer Antumbra had gleaned from a Library of Congress released CD: "Reason Why That Women Is Wiser Than Men (I Yoked Up A Pig)", "Lily of the West" and "Darling, I Have Come to Tell You." The other two songs were from the Woody Guthrie songbook: "Pretty Boy Floyd" and "Dust Can't Kill Me."

The songs were nearly incomparable to their originals, sharing only some of the lyrics and maybe a chord or two. Homer Antumbra had reworked each of the songs into a structure complete in its originality and feel. Bob Dylan had a way of doing this, taking the old and making it new.

This, like *blackblacktheskywasblack*, was a hit for Walter's Glow-In-The-Dark-Skeleton Records, selling completely out of the seven-inch vinyl in less than a week of its release. The band went on another tour, this one two weeks with no breaks between performances, across the Midwest and South. The crowds grew, as did the critical acclaim for both the recordings and the live performances.

"Utterly breathtaking"
—*Uncut Melodic* said of the band's show.

"Soul crushing"
—*Louisville Plugged* said of *blackblacktheskywasblack*.

"Unbelievably imaginative . . . the way the songs should've sounded"—*Orleans Definitive* said of *thesesongsiforgot*.

Between performances, Homer Antumbra wrote and wrote and wrote. He wrote a plethora of new songs, crafting them piecemeal from fragments of his short stories or narrative poetry.

"Homer wrote these simple three chord songs," Harold said. "I mean they were sim-ple. Just the bare essentials were there. The idea and the chords, sometimes not even full chords, sometimes just three notes, and he'd play it for you and it just did something. There was some sort of magic involved. I came to think of the things [songs] more as spells than tunes. Everyone would hear them and know exactly what was required, which was more often than not an overextension of their talents or skillsets, and the music would flow like some deep, dark current.

"Simple though they were, they changed and grew. They became these super intrinsic things of absolute beauty and desolation. We were all under the spell, each of us called to cull what was required from ourselves and throw it on the heaping altar fire."

Over the next five years, the lineup of the band remained the same and the band toured extensively, playing an average of 180 shows per year during that time period. This grueling schedule could shake even a veteran of the touring life but the band performed consistently with very few mishaps.

They also reentered Studio Eh and recorded their haunting sophomore release: *whatwillcomewillcome*. This album sold every bit as well as the their first and the covers EP. The band also garnered quite a bit of airtime on most of the college radio stations. The audience knew the songs and when the song structure and timing hadn't departed too much from the recordings they joined along with Homer Antumbra in singing the lyrics.

"Did you ever cover up the church name and phone number from the van?"

"Hell no. Why the fuck would we've done that?" Hershey Walters said, laughing. "Church vans, next to school buses, are the least likely vehicle for a state trooper to pull over. That prick [Jimmy Ross] eventually gave up calling me about the thing though. I wouldn't doubt it if the bastards changed their phone number because of that van."

Chapter Eight
In Sickness & In Health

> In all the muddle
> There are several
> Deep, enlightening puddles.
> There is light
> And there is the Light.
> There are ways
> And there is the Way.
> The Path has many beginnings
> And middles, but only one end:
> Darkness.
>   —From the notebooks of Homer Antumbra

After five long years of constant touring and all the havoc this can wreak on a person's physical and mental health, especially with a constant stream of alcohol serving as your primary source of hydration, the band was forced to take a break late in the winter of their fifth year together. Homer Antumbra was drinking profusely, from waking until passing out somewhere on the road between shows.

"It was so good for those first few years," Harold said. "I mean, it was tiring but it was great. We were playing to sold out or nearly sold out shows most nights and everybody was at the top of their games. Homer and Angel were drinking more than anybody, more than I'd ever seen anybody drink to be honest with you, but they were holding up their end of the bargain."

"You can only keep up that kind of pace for so long," Steinbeck said. "All the traveling, the shows, the constant demand for perfection, for putting on a show. It can get really overwhelming. Drinking really helped us wind down, stay sane. For a while it did anyway."

The first mention of anything going awfully awry comes from a performance review in the *Johnson City Stage* blog:

> *I'm accustomed to seeing drunk performers. I'm used to seeing drunk performers perform though. There are some really great inebriated acts that make it work, Deer Tick comes to mind, and Homer Antumbra and his band almost lived up to this. It was forty-five minutes of great drunken energy then fifteen minutes of the pisser nodding off. He was dead on his feet. Had to be helped off the stage. It was pitiful.*

The episode must've been significant enough and continued after the show as the next night's concert in Winston-Salem had to be cancelled, citing Homer Antumbra's illness. Yet, the next night in Charlotte, the band played for nearly two and a half hours to a packed house. *The Niner Times*, the college newspaper of the University of North Carolina at Charlotte, said the concert was "amazing . . . dynamic . . . captivating."

"Yeah, we were drinking really, really hard that day," Steinbeck said. "Woke up drinking, skipped breakfast, drank through lunch and on up to the show. When we pulled up to the venue [in Johnson City, Tennessee] we all looked back and saw Ant and knew we were in some trouble. I mean I was drunk but—did you know they call me 'Drunken Angel'? They called me that before the Lucinda Williams song came out and then that just kind of solidified it—I was nearly always drunk then and I knew how to function that way. Ant was different. He wasn't used to having anything asked of him.

"We'd been on the road for like five weeks or something ridiculous by the time this show rolled around and we all needed a break. Ant most of all. You know the songs we were playing, how much they asked of you each time you stepped onto the stage. Well, double or triple that for Ant. I mean he was the emotional center for these soul-twisting, heart-wrenching things, and he had to give everything in him every single night in order for the show to go off."

"We still had three weeks ahead of us at that point [the Johnson City concert]. I guess I did and didn't see it coming," Harold said. "I mean, when you're spending nearly every waking, and non-waking moment at that, with someone, the minute changes in social barometer or someone's inner workings and the outward display of such can go unnoticed. I guess we'd been drinking a bit too much, all of us, for the past week or two leading up to that night but I didn't catch any warning signs at the time. I mean the shows came off strong and didn't seem to be slipping."

"We were just out there being a band on the road, you know?" Lewis said. "Of course we were drinking more than we would had we been home. That's the road. That's roadlife. That's just part of it."

Not a week after the Johnson City show, things got progressively worse for Homer Antumbra and the band.

"We played a show in Norfolk [Virginia] and had to drive all the way to Huntington [West Virginia] for a show the next day and it'd been piss pouring rain all damn night and day," Fulkers said. "Ant was in the back with Angela, sleeping I assumed, Skip was upfront with me, and Mikey was reading some treatise of the Roman Empire or some shit, off in his own world like usual. I don't know where we were. Somewhere up in the foggy mountains of West Virginia, I guess. Well, there's this strangled gasp from the back. Skip turns around and asks what's up but gets no response.

"Angel has this little voice from way back there. I had to turn down the radio—Johnny Cash's *American Recordings*, I remember that's what was on—to hear what she was saying. Her voice was wrong, not just drunk or whatever, but wrong. She said that he'd stopped breathing. Mikey had climbed over the gear to the back by this point and screamed to stop the van, to pull over."

"In recollection, I have no idea why I told 'em to pull over," Harold said. "It just seemed like the natural thing to do, to stop the motion. When somebody is in that kind of trouble, it doesn't feel right for you to be skipping across the land like that. I should've screamed to get us to a hospital."

"We pulled over and spread him out flat on his back across the aisle and Specs started doing CPR, which totally didn't surprise me that he knew how to do that," Lewis said. "Somebody called 911, I can't remember who, must've been Brandon. Lord knows it couldn't have been Angel, she was trashed."

"He was blue. Not just his normal pale, yellowish color but blue. Like a fucking fish," Fulkers said. "I'd never been so scared in my life."

The ambulance arrived and Antumbra was rushed to a hospital in nearby Oak Hill, West Virginia, where he was treated for an overdose and his stomach was pumped.

"Some guy had given them to me after the set in Norfolk," Steinbeck said.

"What were you given?"

"Xanax. This guy gave me an entire bottle of 'em," she said.

"He just gave it to you?" I asked.

"Well, I can be very persuasive," she said.

I've heard Janice Angela Steinbeck referred to as an Amazonian. She's six-feet-two-inches of slim and shapely woman. Long, auburn curls, piercing green eyes and a full mouth; I can see her being very persuasive indeed.

"Is this something that you and Homer had done before?"

"I had. I'm not sure if Homer had. I guess not since he didn't know his limit. Then again, we were all pretty wore down from the road so it could've been that his system was just not in working order enough to pick 'em," Steinbeck said.

The rest of the tour was at first postponed, then cancelled outright as Homer Antumbra spent a week in the hospital recovering.

"They thought he was gonna be in a coma at first," Fulkers said. "I felt like crying when the doctors came out and told us that. We all just sat there. Angel was still wrecked but seemed to be drying up a little. I guess something like that will help to sober you up, at least a little."

"I knew they were doing something back there," Harold said. "The doctors said they found a bunch of pills in him. Little blue pills. There was more giggling than I thought natural for just a normal drunk. Apparently, mixing Xanax with alcohol can cause a euphoric feeling. I sat next to Angel and grilled her about it. She was pissed at first but too strung out to really put up much of a front. I got the bottle from her—it was an entire fucking bottle of some guy's prescription, still had his name and pharmacy info and all that on it—and went to the bathroom and flushed the entire thing."

The next day, the band—minus Brandon Fulkers—drove back to Minneapolis, taking shifts behind the wheel and not stopping for anything other than gas and burgers. Back in the Twin Cities, Lewis went to Hershey Walters' house and broke the news to him personally. They made some calls, postponed the next few tour dates, then when Homer was still in the hospital and in no shape to get back on the road after five days, they cancelled the rest of the dates, citing illness in the band.

Brandon Fulkers stayed with his friend, sleeping in the hospital room for the first two nights and checking into a nearby motel after hospital staff made it known he couldn't continue to do so. Homer improved a little each day but lost almost ten pounds off his already emaciated frame.

"He was so ashamed. I felt bad for him," Fulkers said. "When he came to and I finally got in there to see him, he wouldn't hardly look me in the eyes. He just asked me to find his notebook and a pen and bring them to him. After everyone headed back to the Cities and it was just me and Ant, he opened up like he never did before. He said that life was one struggle after another and he had weakened to the point of doing what he'd done. He apologized, said he knew he let me and the band down.

"It was hard to hear him say it. I mean, I was upset that the rest of the tour had to be cancelled but I needed a break too. Hershey had us running ragged. I told him it was okay and that I'd be there for him and that seemed to really shock something in him. I don't think anybody had ever said that to him before."

When he was well enough for travel, Antumbra and Fulkers flew back to Minneapolis. Homer Antumbra met with Hershey Walters within a few days of arriving home. They discussed the band's immediate touring future and where they would go from there.

"Ant said he didn't want to tour anymore," Walters said. "I asked him if he meant ever and he shook his head but didn't seem real certain. That kind of scared me a bit. I mean that's how records get promoted, you know? Said he needed to take a break but wanted to hit the studio again soon. That gave me a big sigh of relief."

Up to this point, Homer Antumbra and the band had been doing interviews on occasion, with the other members of the band answering the majority of the questions posed and Homer answering only when he was cornered to do so. Requests for interviews after the tour cancellation quadrupled and nearly all of them were declined or granted only with Hershey Walters.

I sent Homer Antumbra an email following the news of the tour's cancellation. He responded within a day but declined to answer the specifics of what was going on with illness in the band. His response, in fact, was a cryptic puzzle including the following:

> *Hope all is well for you and yours. The Path is long,*
> *weary and difficult to trod at times. Sometimes it's lost in*
> *the Darkness. But there is a Light and I will shine it in*
> *sickness & in health.*

He also provided me with another couple of volumes to add to my reading list, including Jonathan Swift's *Gulliver's Travels*, Homer's *Iliad* and *Odyssey* and the more contemporary *The Grapes of Wrath*. All of which, sadly, I hadn't read as of that time.

Homer Antumbra recovered and wrote continuously in the

process. The event helped to shape the songs' structure and tone. They were slower, more extended periods of haunting silence and darker in tone and theme. He did not tour again for nearly five years, instead focusing intently on writing, recording and releasing records, beginning with a string of EPs on, of course, Walters' Glow-In-The-Dark-Skeleton Records.

The band rehearsed three times a week and spent days upon end in Studio Eh, now almost a headquarters for the musicians.

"They were in here all the time. It was wonderful," Jamie Kurtz said. "Not only because it was guaranteed income, which it was, but because they were so open to experimentation and the *sound*. We did all kinds of shit on those recordings that no other band would've even thought, let alone dared, to try."

"Like what?"

"Like setting up in the alley out back and recording the intro and first verse of 'Poisoned' at four in the morning in thirty-degree weather. Like running some vocals through an Orange [guitar amplifier] through a whole maze of mostly guitar effect pedals. Whatever seemed to fit the *sound* or the tone of the song was fair game and I think those records are the strongest sounding as a result."

The band released five EPs, both on seven-inch multi-colored vinyl and CD, during the next three years: *acceptance*; *rage*; *autumnalhymns*; *pathwaysoflight&darkness*; and *ladyatthecrossroads*. Looking back at these records, it's clear the path Homer Antumbra was on artistically. The first of the extended plays, *acceptance*, is a meditation on the choices one can make.

> *There is a right, there is a wrong, there is a light, there is*
> *a long road home.*
> —From "long road home"

A.S. Coomer

Some things must be, some things we'll see.
Others break at the bend of our knees.
—From "mechanized understanding"

The four songs from *acceptance* break down all the world to choices.
There are no-brainers, there are some that are just easier to make
than others. Then there are the ones that define a person, usually a
culmination of conscious act and unconscious will. Homer Antumbra was coming to grips with his place in the world—a musician, a poet, something he swore he'd never become—and the tone
is one of dark acceptance. It is a brooding atmospheric whirl of deep
blues and nearly black purples. The liner notes are snatches of lines
from Arthur Rimbaud, Charles Bukowski, and Leo Tolstoy. The
artwork came from an oil painting Homer Antumbra painted himself, featuring a thick coat of black, bruskly adhered to the canvas
then endeared with a gold semi-ring.

At the time of its release, it outsold anything the band had previously released or had been released on Walters' label in general.

Upon release of the *acceptance* extended play, Homer Antumbra
went right back to writing new songs. The band did not tour. They
played scattered shows in the Twin Cities, mainly at Cliff's Place,
but still practiced at least three times a week. The practices grew to
include friends then friends of friends.

"They [the practice sessions] felt almost like a religious ceremony of
some sort," Fulkers said. "Like it was some Church of the Damned
meeting. At first, it was just us, then some friends started sitting in
and watching. Then more and more people started coming until it
was almost like a show. It was crazy. I don't mean the atmosphere
was wild or anything. In fact, it was very respectful. Specs would
use *reverence* or some such word and he'd be right. Everyone who
came to our practices didn't interrupt us. They didn't get drunk or

94

get loud. They sat and watched and listened. They treated it like it was as important to them as it was to us. And as strange as it seems, none of us were unnerved by a watchful mass of people there, not even Ant."

Hershey Walters pressured the band to tour in support of *acceptance* but Homer Antumbra refused and eventually took on some extra shows around the Cities to appease the label owner. The band went back into Studio Eh and recorded another EP, this one five songs in length and entitled *rage*.

rage was longer in length than *acceptance*, not just because it had one additional song, but because the songs were longer, more expansive, and even more brooding. If *acceptance* was about understanding, *rage* was self-explanatory. The songs were spiteful and bitter, desolate and hopeless, all with an undercurrent of shiftlessness.

> *It wasn't supposed to be this way, it never is.*
> *Walk on out, as is your wont.*
> —From "this way"

> *Ghosts and me, ghosts and me,*
> *a vast panoply of flickering lights.*
> —From "ghosts and me"

> *Become it, becoming it. Become it, becoming it.*
> *Wasteful. Wasted. Waste.*
> —From "become (the fall)"

"ghosts and me" became a top ten hit on the college radio circuit. It's breathy alchemy of silence, whispers, and atmospherics crackled into dorm rooms across the country, fueling even more sales at Glow-In-The-Dark-Skeleton Records. Walters didn't press Antumbra to hit the road as hard, so long as he kept churning out hit records.

And this was something Homer Antumbra did for the entirety of his career. Of course, you must qualify exactly just what a 'hit record' was for the artist and the label. Glow-In-The-Dark-Skeleton Records was (and still is) an indie label. Walters has no major label backing. No major distribution, other than a handful of independent record stores across the Twin Cities and the country. Of course the music has been made available digitally through online retailers and streaming services such as iTunes, Amazon, and Spotify and that has upped sales and notoriety of Antumbra's music and the label tremendously. The label has an online store where customers can purchase the hardcopy versions, both vinyl and compact disc, of the recordings. That being said, a 'hit record' for an indie label and artist isn't anywhere near, probably not even in the same city, county or state of the ballpark, as a major label pop singer. If Madonna released a single that sold as 'well' as any of Antumbra's highest grossing records it would be dubbed an abysmal failure by both the Queen of Pop and her label.

Antumbra and the band wasted no time after the release of *rage*. They served up another dish of five songs on another extended play titled *autumnalhymns*. This set of songs has often been claimed, by fans and several critics alike, to be Antumbra's finest recording. The songs blend the themes and tones of *acceptance* and *rage* perfectly. The EP is the next step forward. The only step the songs of its two predecessors, and the two full-length albums for that matter, along the path that could be taken.

The songs along this path are, paradoxically, both louder and softer than anything that had previously been released from Antumbra. There are soaring, searing guitars then whispered, trance-like dirges. It doesn't play for longer than thirty-five minutes but after that last note fades into oblivion, you feel like you have just completed the longest, most demanding journey of your life. You feel accomplished and destroyed at the same time. A steady inkling that you'll still be 'walking the Path' from this point forward but coupled with an understanding and acceptance that you'll 'never be whole' again are what you take away from the experience.

I think the reason the album is favored so heavily by fans and critics alike is that it is the most succinct expression of the ideals of the man that he ever released. The EPs and albums to come would stretch and explore more fully the themes and undercurrents Antumbra was traversing here and delve into the practice of narrative song structure in the process. *autumnalhymns* is a songbook of Shining the Light, Walking the Path, hopelessness and hauntedness, all the facets of Homer Antumbra's music compressed with the gravity of a singularity into just thirty-five minutes. It is the heaviest, most sincere half hour you can continuously take part in.

After the release of *autumnalhymns*, there was another meeting between Antumbra and Walters regarding touring.

"He said he wasn't going to tour again until he was ready but couldn't—or wouldn't—tell me when that would be," Walters said. "He still didn't look good. I mean, I'm guessing he looked better than when . . . it happened, out there in West Virginia—they said he was blue, blue, can you imagine?—but he still didn't look like a normal, healthy person."

"What made him look unhealthy?"

"He was gaunt. Yellowish, pale, skinny. Like a sick puppy or a Holocaust survivor or something."

"What reasons did he have for not being ready to go back to touring?"

"He said he wasn't ready. Said he had some work to do. I thought he meant a job but the only job he had that I knew of was at Dave Ingles' record store, which was a work-whenever-you-want-to kind of thing. I guess he meant writing the songs. He said he wanted to release another EP and I didn't get back around to asking him about touring again."

The next EP was *pathwaysoflight&darkness*. Here, the narrative poetry from Antumbra's earlier life in Nebraska came back, full force. The songs, though not directly connected, as would be the case with the conceptual albums to come in the next few years, were linked in tone and structure.

"They were story songs," Steinbeck said. "A throwback to the veil. Something to cover up the ideas and present them in a more understanding or unassuming way. Having the songs tell a story opened up the songs to more people. Everybody loves a good story, even one that is nearly incomprehensible or bleak."

pathwaysoflight&darkness was sharply criticized by some fans for its apparent departure from the immediate mode of expression. The songs of earlier, though not necessarily always in a first person point of view, were now shaped in third person and followed a series of events, whether internalized by a character or outwardly in some darkened, midnight land. I never really understood these critiques. I think they stem from a shortcoming—lack of patience, more than anything else—on the part of the critic. The songs still hold true to every song Antumbra has ever written. The tones and themes are forever Antumbra. With this stylistic shift, Antumbra is allowed to paint broad or minute landscapes and scenes with a payoff that comes in the long run as opposed to the short.

The next release, *ladyatthecrossroads*, was the next logical step in the process. This six song extended play is a complete work in its entirety. The songs tell a story, starting with the first track and ending with the last, of a weary, midnight traveler coming to a crossroads in some bleak land and meeting a wolf-headed woman in a red dress. She beckons the traveler to follow, assumingly to his doom, and the traveler is embattled with the decision. He eventually follows the lady at the crossroads and the record ends in a hushed, stygian gloom, signifying the end of the traveler's prior existence.

The record, for Homer Antumbra, signified an end to his prior artistic existence as well. For the next three years, Antumbra would write solely in the narrative format and take up a reaching story arc that spanned six studio albums with *ladyatthecrossroads* serving as a precursor, a prologue of sorts, and a muse to return to halfway through.

Chapter Nine
D ● r k   R i v ● r

I was walking and thinking late into the night. I was crossing the muddy Mississippi on the Stone Arch and Will stood before me; eyes shining in fright and zeal. A zealot of old, hunted and haunted, fleeing and seeking. The Light on one side of the moving, darkened waters, Darkness on the other.

On the banks laden with shadow, eyes followed his movements, waiting on his misstep. On the side in Light, nothing save his dreams of resting in illumination waited.

—From the notebooks of Homer Antumbra

After five straight extended play releases, Hershey Walters wanted nothing more than a tour and a new album from Homer Antumbra and his bandmates. Antumbra still refused to tour but had been crafting the framework for an epic series of conceptual albums, originally planned to be four in total but expanded to six in final, and eventually outlined the narrative to Walters.

"Initially, I admit, I wasn't super excited," Walters said. "Concept albums are an iffy business, even when they're good—and that's not that often—but a string of them was tantamount to career suicide, sales suicide. The idea seemed dead in the womb to me.

"I was wrong. Not the first time that's happened and probably won't be the last."

"You said 'initially'. What changed your mind during the process?"

"The songs," Walters answered immediately. "I didn't hide my trepidation. He told me to come out and watch a practice—tons of people did that every week, which was insane—and I did. They played the songs and I couldn't believe it but they were on par or better than what they'd played up to that point. I was sold."

"He sat us down and started in on this story," Skip Lewis said. "No preface. No 'this is going to be our work for the next three years, our next six full-length studio releases.' We were all setting up for practice and he just asked us to listen for a minute and we did. He talked about Will as if he were a guy we all knew, a friend. By the time he got to the end, we were mystified. It was a crazy story, something very familiar about it though."

"I was just standing there with my mouth hanging open after he finished," Steinbeck said. "I asked him what he had just read and could I borrow that book, it just sounded so gripping. Then he said it was going to be the story we were going to tell."

"Fuck, man," Fulkers said. "I had never been so excited to be a part of something. So glad I'd joined the band. So glad I had come across Ant and had the opportunity to make music with him. Will's story should've been a daunting task, probably would've been to any other musician in any other band—but it wasn't to me or anybody else in our band. It was like we all understood that this was the next step. The other recordings, the other songs were in preparation for this larger, more complex and complete work. We were all super excited to get to work."

And they had their work cut out for them. Antumbra told his bandmates and label boss the bare bones of the story but was still fleshing out the details. He had a beginning, a middle, and an end in the most simplistic of terms and felt the rest would come out as the band shaped the sounds. He was right. He also worked tirelessly on the narrative for nearly every minute of every day. He took long walks late into the night, often coming back to the Stone Arch Bridge and stopping halfway across to stare down into the ever-moving waters of the mighty Mississippi.

He also drank more and more often but kept it from interfering with his work for the most part. None of his bandmates said Homer drank at their practice sessions, which were used primarily for writing both the songs and narrative details, nor did he show up inebriated. It seems the work was enough to keep Homer Antumbra on the wagon, at least during business hours.

I know I said in the introduction that this biography would not include a track-by-track analysis of Antumbra's work. I will stick to this declaration (I hope to take up this charge in another book in the future!) but the story unfolding over the course of these six albums is essential for a complete understanding and appreciation of the artist. Though I will not break each track down individually, over this section of the book I will cover the story told by the songs extensively. The themes and stylistic variation between the albums are varied and awe inspiring. The scope and execution of the work makes these six albums collectively into Homer Antumbra's magnum opus.

The story's protagonist, Will, embarks on a monomythic journey that can be elucidated with Joseph Campbell's hero's journey, *The Hero With A Thousand Faces* or Christopher Vogler's interpretation of Campbell's work, *The Writer's Journey*. I'm going to break down the six-album masterwork into the basic three-act structure and outline the twelve stages of Will's journey. In doing this, I'm going to side-step the tedious track-by-track explanation I've promised to avoid and retell the story of the six albums as a short story reworking. I'm going to try and capture the subtle tones of the music and paint it in the same dark hues of blue and black that you hear on the recordings.

Act One
Album One: *midnightland*

Ordinary World: Will awakes to the darkness. He spends his days in it. When he closes his eyes to sleep he can barely tell the difference between the world outside his head and the world within.

"Midnightland, Midnightland," he whispers.

Then one night he has the dream. The sky opens and distinguishes itself from the darkness.

"There is Light. There is Light," he sings.

When he opens his eyes in the morning, all remains dark.

Call to Adventure: Having seen the Light, all of Will's waking thoughts and his dreams are consumed by it. He feels the warmth on his face, his head upturned to the Light, eyes closed. He finds himself staring up at the empty sky more and more often, wishing, hoping, longing for the Light.

He dreams there is a land where the sun shines, a land of Light.

Refusal of the Call: Will longs for the Light but finds setting out on a search for it too much to bear. Creature comforts are hard to leave for the life of a traveler. Though he has no family or companions, he has a bed and a small shack that he built with his own hands. There are the barren fields to tend and the darkness is all he's ever known.

A.S. Coomer

<u>Meeting With The Mentor</u>: Will wakes in the night. An unnatural desire to move overtakes him and he can't find sleep. He leaves his dwelling and seeks the road. He walks and walks and walks until he is further from his home than he has ever been. He comes to a crossroads. Something pricks at his skin, some invisible electricity, and he knows he is not alone and that something is going to happen.

Out of the darkness, the Lady in Red materializes. She crosses into the middle, where the two roads meet, and beckons him forward. Will cannot resist and finds his feet moving on their own accord.

<u>Crossing the Threshold</u>: Will stands before the Lady in Red and finds himself floored by his sudden nakedness, goosebumps and shivering rack his thin, frail body.

"You seek the Light?" she asks.

Will cannot find his voice. He nods his head and cowers from her hard eyes.

"The vile Light will destroy you, consume you," she says.

And Will knew it to be true. Something deep in his stomach drops and he feels lost, embarrassed at his incapacity to understand.

"Follow me. I will show you how to walk in the shadows," the Lady in Red says.

Will follows her across the two adjoined roads off into the darkness.

Act Two

Album Two: *aworldofdarkness*

<u>Tests, Allies, Enemies</u>: She offers him her hand. Will takes it. The Lady in Red moves in a glide; there are no jerks, no steps. Will struggles to keep up.

"Light is futile," she tells him. "Darkness comes to all in the End."

Will knows this, somewhere deep inside his stomach where he

thinks his heart used to be, and shame floods his face when he re-calls feeling the Light from the sky warm his eyelids.

"Foolish things come and go but the Darkness remains," she tells him.

Will nods his head.

"There is a body of water that understands, that cuts through the world," she tells Will. "You will cross the Dark River and all will be understood."

Will sleeps and wakes to thoughts of the Dark River, of seeking it, finding it. He dreams he is wading out into its black waters and all is finally understood.

The Lady in Red teaches him the Words and sets him on his travels: to rectify the lunacy of the Light; to help the people understand the workings of the world. She gives him a ring of obsidian, the blackest of blacks Will has ever seen. He dreams of the river, of wading out into the middle and seeing the other side.

Album Three: *darkwaters*

Approach: The Lady in Red comes and goes. Will combs the countryside, preaching the Darkness.

"Have you dreamt about the Light?" he asks the farmers, the townsfolk, the children. "Have you felt its shameful warmth on your sleeping cheeks?"

He sees some heads nodding but mostly a quiet reservation that tells him they had.

"It's a lie," Will says. "It will betray you. It will lift you up into the sky, sure, but it will leave you in the end. We come into Dark-ness, we will leave in it too. You'll find nothing but shame in the Light. Shame and disappointment and betrayal."

He sees the tears but knows it's better to live in the rational than in mirage. Better crack the heart now when it can heal than crush it in the delusions of the Light in the end, when no time for repair remains.

"Better now than then," Will whispers.

In the midnightland sky, walking through the fields and forests, the sad, smiling moon stares down.

Time ceases to matter for Will. He travels and travels, preaching all the while. He notes pains in his knees in the mornings and back at night. He's getting older, he realizes one night. He's getting older and doesn't feel any more whole than he used to. He dreams of the Dark River and in the morning finds himself standing at its shore.

He strips off his ragged clothes and steps into the black, moving water. He wades until he's waist deep and through the heavy mist he can just make out the shore on the other side. Another step finds the water chest high and the next over his head. The water fills his nose and mouth and eyes. He can't see anything but the Darkness, can't feel anything but the cold. The taste is bitter and metallic. He struggles against the water but it is strong. He is overwhelmed and suddenly realizes he can't tell which way is forward, which way is up, which is down. He is lost in the Dark River.

His feet scrape the bottom and he realizes a black blacker than that surrounding him is emanating just in front of his eyes. It takes a few moments but he realizes it's the ring the Lady in Red has given him. He feels a pull at his hand and the ring leads him across the river bottom to the shore on the other side.

He comes from the Dark River naked and shivering. He realizes he hasn't drowned, hasn't swallowed any amount of water that he can tell. He was simply washed and carried away by the Darkness. He steps into the forest and sets about preaching the Darkness, a newfound sense of gratefulness glowing like embers in his stomach.

Album Four: *steppingfromthedarkness*

<u>Central Ordeal</u>: But it didn't last long. Will came to see the hopelessness of the people and realized the gratefulness at surviving

the Dark River was something akin to disappointment and confusion. Hadn't he sought the Light? Why had he chosen the Darkness? What good was a life without Light?

The Lady in Red came to him at night but he shielded himself from her in ways he hadn't before. He refused to look her in the eyes and he only half listened to her words. The Father in Flowing Robes, a tall, gaunt man in black, emerges from the shadows and preaches the Darkness to Will. The Father in Flowing Robes' eyes and sharpened teeth tell Will that his decisions come with consequences, that he has been given a path and to step away from it would bring trouble.

He, again, dreamed of the Light. It flooded through the Darkness and upturned the corners of his lips and he found his face wet with warm tears. When he woke the Lady in Red sat before him with hard, watching eyes.

He continued his preaching and traveling but his heart wasn't in it. His words rang out hollow and empty. He saw the Dark River in his mind's eye and knew he would need to cross it again to seek the Light.

Seizing the Sword: His dreams swirled and clouded over in electric Light and the fog shielded off the Darkness. He felt himself in a cocoon of understanding. He had a flame in himself, a Light of his own. He would Shine his Light when he came to, he would Shine his light and forsake the Darkness.

She was there when he woke. She and the Father in Flowing Robes but Will didn't see him until afterwards. The Lady in Red asked Will to pledge his commitment to the Darkness. She brings him to the small child on the hill. She gives Will the dagger and tells him to slay the girl.

"She is spreading betrayal. Telling the people that the Light must be shined," The Lady in Red says.

Will takes the dagger and hesitates over the child.

"She can't be more than nine," he says.

The Lady in Red's face hardens and the Father in Flowing Robes steps from the forest.

"You must not allow the lies of the Light to poison the people," he says.

It doesn't feel right. Will can't bring himself to even consider doing what he has been asked to do. Will remembers the Light on his face and feels shame that he abandoned his search for it. He feels sick knowing how many people he'd preached the Darkness to. Will realizes he must seek out the Light and Shine his own.

He flings the dagger from the hill and pulls the girl to her feet, fleeing into the night. They run for days until they find the girl's family and she is returned. Will is hunted. The Lady in Red, the Father in Flowing Robes, packs of wolves, all seek his death. He has betrayed them. He must die.

Act Three

Album Five: *returning*

The Road Back: Will flees his pursuers and seeks out the Dark River. He is chased and nearly caught several times. A great serpent-headed hydra appears to him in his dreams and he slays it after an exhausting battle. He wakes to find the wounds he took in his sleep are present on his body upon waking.

He comes to a high plain and sees the Dark River flowing below. Behind him, a horde of the Darkness is gaining, led by the Lady in Red and the Father in Flowing Robes. The Father in Flowing Robes somehow overtakes Will and the two fight as the legion quickly gains on them. Will trips the Father in Flowing Robes as he lunges at him with his sword and Will flees across the plains but not before suffering several lacerations and one deep puncture wound in his left arm.

Album Six: *aplaceinthelight*

Climax: Will descends to the Dark River and finds a raven-headed ferryman untying his boat. Will begs the man to take him across the raging river, which is impassable and erupting in torrents and great rapids at this section. The ferryman asks for money, of which Will has none, but sees the ring of obsidian on his finger and agrees to take Will across in exchange for it. Will agrees, hands the ring over, and they set off just as Will's pursuers come to the shore.

Halfway across, the ferryman loses his resolve at seeing the Lady in Red and the Father in Flowing Robes shouting and cursing for Will to be handed over. He begins to turn the ferry around but Will struggles to stop him and the raven-headed ferryman pulls his sword from his scabbard and gives Will the choice to return to the shore of the Shadow, where the Lady in Red and Father in Flowing Robes were waiting, watching, or jump into the Dark River.

Will chooses to jump into the turbulent water and is quickly swept away. He crashes into rocks, is sucked down by undercurrent, then spit up briefly only to be pulled back under. He fights the water, trying desperately to get to the other side, the side he left so long ago. He fights until he has no strength left and is swept under one last time, knowing that he abandoned the Light and would no longer Shine his own. The last fleeting image in Will's mind is a candle quickly flickering out.

Denouement: The raven-headed ferryman returns to the shore, wearing the obsidian ring, with his head bowed, mumbling apologies to the Lady in Red and the Father in the Flowing Robes. The ferryman swears that he didn't know who he was carrying across the river, didn't know that he was wanted. The ferryman said when he got halfway across he heard their calls and made to turn the boat around and return to the shore but the man had fought him and leapt into the river.

The Lady in Red sees her black ring on the ferryman's finger and nods to the Father in Flowing Robes, who takes hold of the boatman and slashes his throat with a black dagger. The Lady in Red removes her ring and the wolves tear into the raven-headed corpse.

Miles downstream, where the Dark River widens and its current slows, Will's body washes ashore. It sits there overnight and in the morning a beautiful young woman in a white gown, coming down to the shore to retrieve some of the bitter water for her father to make brandy wine, finds him. She rushes to his side and finds him long dead, his body cold and his skin blue. She runs to her father and together they bury the body just inside a clearing some yards from the bank. She cries for the stranger, whose face she finds hard but kind, and covers his grave with the smoothest, shiniest river rocks. Days pass and great blooms of flowers cut through the sodden earth.

Well, there's my brief synopsis of what fans call "The Dark River Chronicles." It is, of course, nowhere near as powerful or moving as the recordings themselves. Music has always had a one-up on the written word. What are poems but attempts at the a cappella? Music set to speech.

Each of the Dark River albums has a feel, theme, and direction completely its own. Any one of them could stand up to any of the more heralded concept albums and equal or, in my opinion, easily surpass them. What is the self-exploratory *Ziggy Stardust* compared to the desperate soul-searching of *steppingfromthedarkness?* Or the experimentation of *The Dark Side of the Moon* to the hazy, bleak soundscape of *aplaceinthelight?* Listeners will have to judge for themselves. I trust anyone serious enough to put the Dark River Chronicles on the turntable will understand.

The theme of *midnightland* is wariness. Will is stuck in infinite repeat in a world of the mundane. The tone of this album is that of the doldrums. Everything is the same, nothing changes. Will yearns for escape. The spirit shifts when the Light shines on Will in his dreams. The tone becomes murky with the appearance of the Lady in Red. Will's choice to follow her off into the shadows ends the record in a whisper of discordance.

aworldofdarkness is by far the hardest listen of the Chronicles. Hardest as in *War and Peace* is the hardest read of Tolstoy's novels. The album is darkness incarnate. Whole songs devoted to giving up, quitting. Nihilism in musical expression. This is the album that is hard to stare down but everyone should. It shows you something inherent in each of us, that desire to quit, to give up, to accept that one day all will be over and the scorecards won't matter. There is not one strand of hope on the thing. The Dark River is yearned for but Will understands it will only help with acceptance of the hopelessness of the universe, not provide a meaning.

darkwaters picks up where *aworldofdarkness* left off. Emptiness reigns and the music of the album picks up pace in parts to reflect the motion of the story. Once the river is crossed, the music swells and the hopelessness is coupled with heavy, discordant droning.

steppingfromthedarkness marks a significant departure sonically for the band. There is much more raw emotion in this album. The hopelessness is transformed into a crashing uncertainty and ends in a shameful regret that marches on toward what must be. There is a stoic energy to the songs echoing Will's journey and coming around to a mounting fear of the doom nipping at his heels.

returning is an album of devotion. A hard, embattled devotion to seeking the Light and making amends for his doomspeak. Will is constantly pursued and the music takes on a haunted and hunted air as a result. This album clashes and rages and runs scared from start to finish.

aplaceinthelight is the climactic ending to the saga. It feels every bit the last fleeting moments of an embattled life. The betrayal of the ferryman, the torrent of the Dark River, the struggle then the grasp of defeat are all there. It is a somber listen. The brief ending sheds a bittersweet note but the end is the end. It is not a storybook ending. There is no happy Disney flavoring to be found. Will dies knowing he forsake what he sought. The flowers on his grave have the poetic sense of a urinal cake being dropped into an overflowing port-o-john.

The thing is heavy. I've listened to it from start to finish on several occasions and each time walked away exhausted. It hits me everywhere at the same time. I understand the hope, the hopelessness, the yearning, the calamity; it's life. It's everything. It's all there. It hits you like a wave and washes over you, leaving you soaked to the bone. Sure it hurts like hell, but life does too. Don't believe all that shit about 'what doesn't kill you, makes you stronger'. This won't kill you nor will it make you stronger from having heard it but it sure will make you look at things differently. And for the vast majority of those, like me, who find themselves often at a loss, searching, alternately, for the Light or the Darkness, different is good. Different can be life changing. Different can bring a breath of fresh air to a stagnant midnightland.

"It was a fucking whirlwind," Angela Steinbeck said. "We were in the studio nearly every day, it felt like. A lot of what you hear was worked out on the spot. We had the narrative, Ant's story, and a few chords or notes and we worked the rest out with the tape running."

"They were a driven band fronted by a driven man," Jamie Kurtz said. "They all came into the studio with serious faces and there was really minimum cutting up happening during the sessions. I don't think any of them were having 'fun' in the normal sense. They all knew they were working on something special and didn't want to fuck it up."

"When I got the master of *midnightland* I was scared shitless," Herschel Walters said. "I mean, it was good. Really good. But I just kept listening to it and thinking it was too dense, you know? I was afraid it would be too much for a lot people."

As I sat in front of Hershey Walters, I thought: this is record label speak for 'I don't hear a single'.

"But in this business you gotta have trust," Walters said. "I trusted Ant. If anybody stuck with the kid it was me. I put out everything he ever done."

"It was an amazing blur," Brandon Fulkers said. "We worked hard every day. Ant quit working at the record store. Steiner stopped picking up shifts at that crummy bar where she was waitressing. We all up and quit our jobs and spent those three years worrying about the songs more than where our food was going to come from."

"I had Mary, my wife, cook something up for every session, which was something like three or four nights a week," Kurtz said. "Some soup or casserole or something. I don't think they would've eaten if she wouldn't have cooked. It was like they were junkies to the project. Food, sleep, all that was secondary to getting their musical fix."

There have been several attempts over the years since the release of the first album in the Dark River Chronicles to interview Homer Antumbra about the characters and their origins. All have failed miserably, mine included. There was something about the narrative that was supposed to speak for itself. To elaborate would take away the power of the piece. Homer Antumbra refused to talk about it, for one, because he hated interviews. The other reason is the sense of solidarity with those characters. They existed in the Dark River world, in midnightland. To talk about them outside of it, as if they were but names instead of the flesh and blood Antumbra saw them as, would prove nothing less than a betrayal.

Hershey Walters had nothing to worry about with the sales of *midnightland* or any of the rest of the Dark River Chronicles. They outsold anything Antumbra had released in the past. Upon its re-lease, *aplaceinthelight* even popped up in the Billboard Top 200 at 179. This is quite an accomplishment for a band that had no press kits, no high-power PR people, no advertising to speak of besides their touring and word of mouth. Glow-In-The-Dark-Skeleton Rec-ords, at that time particularly, was a tiny indie label with no major distribution. They had a webstore where orders were filled by Her-shey himself or, on occasion, with the help of Antumbra and his bandmates.

Critical praise was nearly universal for every one of the Dark River Chronicles albums. The only slight exception was a few re-views of *aworldofdarkness*. Joel Seward, of the *Roving Gambler Review* (now defunct), and Martie Collinsworth, of the *On A Whim* blog (also now defunct), said this record was too dark, too hopeless, too nihilistic. Each of these critics' viewpoints can be summed up by Collinsworth's line, "As solid as the music is, it's hard to get behind something that keeps reminding you that there's no hope to be had." What both critics failed to realize was they were taking the album out of the context of the work at large. Sure, *aworldofdarkness* was a droning, doomspeak calamity filled LP. That was its purpose. That being said, the music is another facet of the human perspec-tive. It is another integral part of human nature. The songs are hopeless, meaningless, but that pessimism exists.

All of this being said, it is no wonder these two critics took the album out of context, especially if the album's liner notes were skipped or skimmed over. There was no story arc press, nothing to tell the listener or the reviewer that what he was listening to was part of a much larger narrative. The knowing was in the careful lis-tening and reading of the liner notes, of seeing the band perform, of listening to the fanfare and buzz surrounding the work.

"It's really quite strange looking back on all that now," Stephen Michael Harold said. "We were in the thick of it, as they say. We worked on the verse, the chorus, the bridge, the songs, the albums, then moved on to the next. We really didn't hear or seek out any critiques regarding those six recordings. The process was paramount, not the reception."

"What was the band dynamic like during those years?" I asked.

"It was really intense," he said. "We all got along, there was never any issues related to that. We were all just so involved with what we were working on that we'd watch each other and that careful scrutiny over the course of three years can really lead to some weird inner workings in a group like ours."

"What do you mean?"

"Well, for one, we could intuit each other's moods, what we were going to play, what we were going to contribute. We shortcutted each other. I remember Ant played "Father in Flowing Robes" for us for the first time and as he was still going through it for us for the first time, he stopped and looked up at me and said, 'I know what you're thinking. Try a roll instead.' Then he picked the song back up right where he left off and finished it. I had been considering a kind of step on the snare for the part he had been playing but tried the roll instead and it worked out much better than I would've thought. We worked like that the entire time."

"Things got heavy when we heard Cash was going to record 'Loveless'. I mean, Johnny-fucking-Cash, you know?" Steinbeck said. "We were knee deep in *aplaceinthelight* when Hershey showed up at the studio, which was weird because it was really early in the session. He came bustling in, all red-faced, and shouted that Johnny Cash's agent just called and asked if he could record 'Loveless' for his next American Recording release, which was to be produced by Rick fucking Rubin.

"My jaw fucking dropped. I looked over at Ant who was still fiddling with the lyrics for whatever song we were working on, I can't remember which anymore. Hershey thought that Ant didn't hear him so he said it again and Ant just looked up and said, 'Okay. We're kind of working on something right now. Could we talk about this later?' We were all fucking floored. Hershey's fat face blanched and he just turned and stalked out of the place. We got back to work and didn't talk about it again until we were done for the night."

Cash did indeed record "Loveless" for *American III: Solitary Man* but it did not make the final release of the album. This is unfortunate because the recording is every bit as commanding as Cash's cover of Bonnie 'Prince' Billy's "I See A Darkness" and would've added another element of stark reality to the album. The recording of "Loveless" has long since circulated around the web as an unauthorized bootleg and is highly sought after. I've also heard grumblings from certain record label owners that the rights to the recording are being bargained for but the talks have stalled. This, of course, was told to me off the record.

PART THREE

DEATHS, SMALL, LARGE, ALL

Chapter Ten
Annie & Abi

The band finally hit the road again upon the release of *aplaceinthe-light*. Homer Antumbra felt drained after the three intense years of painstaking recording and crafting of the songs of the Dark River Chronicles. He got together with Hershey Walters and the two set up a five-week tour in support of the album that started and ended in Toledo, Ohio.

"We were like, Toledo?! What the hell?" Steinbeck said, laughing. "We'd never even stopped there. I don't think I'd ever been to To-ledo. Maybe drove through on the way up to Detroit on earlier tours but it was nothing to write home about, you know?"

Toledo, Ohio would serve as the beginning and ending of the *aplaceinthelight* tour because a young woman had written to Hershey Walters, care of Glow-In-The-Dark-Skeleton Records, regarding the Homer Antumbra releases. Annie Smallwood had first heard the band playing in the local record store, Culture Clash. As the story goes, Annie Smallwood was in the store to pick up Will Oldham's *Guarapero/Lost Blues 2*, which had recently been restocked at the store and one of the employees had dropped the needle on the *au-*

tumnalhymns EP. Annie was hooked from then on, leaving that day with the EP in hand.

[I've had a rocky time with Annie Smallwood, much like everybody else I've talked to about her. It comes with the territory, which I think you'll understand as this chapter progresses. Here's what you need to know right now: I interviewed Smallwood on several occasions but months prior to the release of this book, she decided that she wanted to be reimbursed for her interviews. I refused and she said I could not quote her.]

Annie Smallwood bought everything Antumbra released and sent a letter to Walters informing him that she would be glad to book a Toledo date if the band ever needed one. She also offered to house and feed the band if they came to town. Walters wrote back and the two kept up the conversation during the three years Antumbra and the band were making the Dark River Chronicles. Walters then forwarded Annie Smallwood's contact info to Antumbra.

Homer Antumbra did not speak of Annie, at least not to reporters, interviewers, music critics, or me. What I have learned I have learned the hard way, through research, Antumbra's notebooks, and interviews with those around them.

"God, she was a fucking nightmare," Steinbeck said of Annie Smallwood. "She came on like she loved the music, and I think at one point she probably did, but by the end of it, she was a controlling, junkie bitch."

"I'm not sure what happened between them," Walters said. "She helped us out with the *aplaceinthelight* tour and I guess Ant and her hit it off and started dating soon after. He moved to Toledo and they got a little place together. I don't know if they moved in together because they were just really serious about each other or because Annie got pregnant."

"That first night of the tour she was very welcoming," Skip Lewis said. "She came on strong and had some drugs. Ant had a problem saying no. By the time the tour was over, he was speaking to her every day on the phone and we ended the thing back in Toledo, staying at Annie's place. He didn't stay on the couch or the living room floor with the rest of us that night."

Homer Antumbra returned to the Twin Cities after the tour but not for very long. He moved to Toledo, Ohio and rented a small two-story house on South Avenue, in which Annie Smallwood soon joined him.

"We didn't know what to think," Steinbeck said. "We had been spending nearly every minute of every day together, working, writing, playing music, then he just up and moved. Didn't tell any of us. I called him and he said he was sitting at the house and I was like what house? That's how we found out he moved to Toledo.

"I was pissed. I thought he was dropping the band for some silly bitch. I think we all thought that. That's what it felt like."

"I assumed we were finished," Harold said. "Ant moved in with Annie Smallwood and didn't clue us in to anything different. We stopped practicing and playing every day. I guess it should've felt more like a sabbatical or something but it didn't. In retrospect, I can see how anyone would need a breather after those three years. I don't think any of us realized how hard they were on us."

"We'd go from drinking every night, maybe popping some pills after the sessions to 'maybe we can practice next week,'" Steinbeck said. "I couldn't have felt shittier about the way things were going."

Homer Antumbra had increasingly been into prescription drugs, particularly anti-anxiety and pain medications. Annie Smallwood was also a frequent user.

"I went out to visit him and see if he was still working on anything, see if we were still gonna be a band, but mostly just to see him," Steinbeck said. "I drive all the way to Toledo in the van and when I finally found the shithole of a house he was living in, he answers the door with fucking Xanax dripping out of his nose. Looked like he sucked off a Smurf, his upper lip was coated in booger-chunked blue. And Annie was in worse shape, if you can believe that."

"Steiner worked it out so that we'd go practice in this creepy church basement in Toledo once a week, which was shitty because we all lived in Minneapolis and only Ant lived in Toledo," Lewis said. "The resentment grew and grew until it felt like we cared more about the band than he did. We were putting in more work than he was. His song output had dwindled until we were mostly reworking old songs or working on covers at the practice sessions instead of working on anything new."

I heard the relationship between Annie Smallwood and Homer Antumbra was often turbulent and sometimes violent. On a whim, I went down to the County Clerk's office and found several police reports, restraining orders, domestic violence protection orders and the like on file. In their first year living together in Toledo, the police were called out to their home and reports were filed on seven separate occasions. All involved 'intoxicated parties', most of the time both Smallwood and Antumbra being under the influence and out of control. Charges of domestic violence, destruction of property, harassment, assault, resisting arrest, public intoxication, and disturbing the peace graced these reports.

Most of the charges were later dropped but the assault charge against Annie Smallwood was carried out by the state and she was convicted and given time served and probation. According to the police report and court documents, Annie Smallwood smashed a half-full vodka bottle over Homer Antumbra's head, causing him to suffer a severe laceration and mild concussion, for which he was hospitalized but left AMA.

"They fought like fucking cats and dogs," Steinbeck said. "Every time she [Smallwood] came to our practices, which I hated that she would even be there, they would inevitably get into some squabble about something stupid."

"What kinds of things did they fight about around you all?" I asked.

"Anything and everything. One time, we were working on this song—that, of course, never made it to any record—that I had come up with the lyrics for," Steinbeck said. "This was unusual for us, as Ant usually handled all that but I had been knocking this thing around for a while and since Ant didn't have anything new to give, we thought we'd give it a go. Anyway, it was a story song of sorts about a little boy that loses his mother and can't find her or his way home. I thought it was going to be something short but poignant. Annie said she didn't want Ant singing it. Said it wasn't up to his level. I thought I was going to gouge her fucking eyes out."

"God, that was a terrible afternoon," Lewis said. "I don't know why Annie Smallwood thought she had any place at our practices but there she was and Steiner had this song we were fucking around with and Annie just couldn't keep her trap shut. Kept making these little snide remarks and, after a bit, Steiner just got sick of it and I thought she was going to tear Annie apart. Lord knows she could've done it. That was the last practice session we had. I hate that it ended like that. Hate it."

"Looking back, I guess I should have seen it coming from a mile away," Fulkers said. "We weren't getting together like we used to, not coming up with the same quality of stuff. Ant just seemed burned out. I guess every band has a shelf life and ours was just up. We were stagnant, sour. And Steiner trying to attack Annie Smallwood was the last straw. Ant just cut us out of his life. Just like that. He left the church basement and we never played together again."

Not three months later, Annie Smallwood found out she was pregnant with Homer Antumbra's child.

> *The bottom dropped out of everything today. All of the import I had placed seemed, suddenly, to be misplaced. All the scurrying across the country to play for the people that, mostly, don't understand. All the scrutinizing over the right tone for my guitar, the right amount of reverb on the right mic. It's all misplaced. I'm going to be a father. Annie is going to have my baby. I can't help hoping for a son but I will love a daughter just the same. I won't lie and say I was positively excited about this from the get go. I don't think Annie saw anything hopeful in my face when she told me this afternoon but I've come to accept it as the next step along the Way. I'm going to be the father my father never was.*
> —From the diary of Homer Antumbra

With the news of Annie Smallwood's pregnancy, a great change came over Homer Antumbra.

"He called me up and said it was over. He said he didn't think he'd ever tour again," Fulkers said. "Told me that Annie was pregnant and that he was going to be a father. He said that he didn't want to miss any part of his child's life, so touring was out of the question.

"It hurt but what can you really say to that? I think I just said

'Okay, Ant. Congratulations,' and hung up. I was devastated."

"Bran [Brandon Fulkers] called me and told me that Annie was knocked up and Ant said he was done touring," Steinbeck said. "My first thought was that it wasn't Ant's. That junkie whore probably had her legs wrapped around any willing cretin in Toledo."

"Brandon came into the store and told me that Ant was going to be a father and said he no longer was going to go out on tour," Walters said. "I was unpacking a box of one hundred *aplaceinthelight* shirts that had just come in. I looked down at the shirts and thought, 'How the hell am I going to move these then?'"

"Did you call him?" I asked.

"You bet your ass I did," he said. "I picked up the phone with Brandon still standing there with that hangdog face. Ant didn't pick up but I left him a real nasty message. 'I know you're going to be a daddy but there are other people counting on you too,' that sort of thing."

"When I heard that Ant was going to be a father and no longer had any interest in touring my immediate question was: what about recording?" Harold said. "I got his number from Bran and called him. He was excited about the pregnancy, which was an excellent response to a hard situation if you ask me. He told me that he couldn't go on tour once the child was born because he didn't want to be an absent father. He hinted that that's the childhood father figure he had: the absent one. I asked him if he still wanted to make music, make records, and he snorted and said 'Of course' like it was the stupidest question I could've asked. Needless to say, I felt relieved."

Annie Smallwood was no stranger to pregnancy. She had become pregnant three times in the past, one of which she carried to full term, delivered, and then had removed by social services. Her parental rights were terminated and the child was adopted by a foster family on the opposite side of the state. Annie Smallwood was, also, no stranger to drugs and run-ins with the law.

Her arrest record—just in Toledo—was colorful and extensive. She'd been picked up several times for shoplifting, passing bad checks, public intoxication, resisting arrest, and possession. She was also charged with child abuse for issues surrounding her drug use while pregnant but the charge was reduced and the child was found to have been dependent, a legalese term meaning the child was determined to have been neglected but no legal fault was found with the parent.

When she became pregnant with Antumbra's child, Annie Smallwood was adamant about having all her prenatal care in neighboring Michigan, to avoid Toledo social services. It's unclear how much of this information Antumbra knew about Smallwood at the time. I'm guessing next to nothing from his upbeat conversations with his bandmates and notebook entries.

Over the course of the pregnancy, Antumbra continued to write and record music, mostly on his four-track in the basement of his house on South Avenue. The songs he wrote during this time stand in stark comparison to the output from before. The songs were filled with a hope that nearly glitters at times. The songs were more personal, less reliant on a narrative.

> *When it shines*
> *I'll let it shine.*
> *No more shadows,*
> *No more run and hide.*
> *Shape the time, Shape the world,*
> *Walk the Path, Light adored.*
>   —From "Light Adored"

Despite his optimism, the relationship remained rocky. There were more incidents with the police, including three arrests for Antumbra with charges including public intoxication, resisting arrest, domestic violence, and disturbing the peace. Most of the charges were dismissed but the domestic violence charge was enough to get Toledo social services involved with the couple, much to the chagrin of Smallwood.

"They were out of control. Out of control," Jackie Dominguez, the couples' next-door neighbor, said. "I mean this isn't the best of places, it is *South* Avenue, but they were all the time yellin' and cussin' and throwing stuff out the windows."

"Does any single event stick out in your mind?" I asked.

She paused and then nodded her head vehemently.

"Yes, yes. This one time they were both good and drunk or high or something, out of whack, and the lady, Ann, comes flying out of the house with the skinny man's guitar," Mrs. Dominguez said. "When he came out behind her she swung it at him. Didn't hit him but it was enough to keep him away. She was cussin' him and he was tryin' to speak calmly, calm her down, but she wasn't having it. She stomped across that yard and smashed the guitar into the trunk of a tree. Smashed it to bits. Craziest thing I've seen on South with my own two eyes. The whole neighborhood was out just watching it too."

"He called me from jail a few times. Once I had the money to bail him out, so I did," Steinbeck said. "Toledo is full of bail bonds people. It's disgusting. Flashing lights in storefronts for 'em. That place is a real shithole. Anyway, the junkie bitch had smashed his Gibson and somehow got Ant arrested for public intoxication in the process. I bailed him out and started to hit the highway towards Minneapolis but he wouldn't let me drive him out of town. Said he had a responsibility to her [Smallwood]. I told him that he didn't owe that crazy bitch shit but he wasn't having it. He was real serious about that baby. Real serious," she said. "He made me turn the car around and take him to the shelter on Cherry Street. He spent the night like a fucking hobo because of that junkie bitch."

> *The Path is hard,*
> *Hardened by the feet of millions,*
> *Hardened by the feet of a million me's.*
> *I've been here before, I've walked this Path.*
> *I know where it leads.*
> —From the notebooks of Homer Antumbra

> *I don't know how it's going to work but it will work. It*
> *will. I will make it work. I will not not be in my child's*
> *life. I will make her understand. I will stand by her, I*
> *will take the venom, I will not cry out, I will not.*
> —From the notebooks of Homer Antumbra

"I went down there at least once a week to work on new material," Fulkers said. "Sometimes Steiner would come along, sometimes not. She really had it in for Annie. The closer Annie got to her due date the more strung out Ant was. He was really messed up near the end. He wasn't even trying to hide it anymore."

"We were working and had been at it for a few hours, empties all around us, and still hitting the wall," Steinbeck said. "Ant stood up, reached into his pocket, and pulled out a handful of Xanax. No bottle. No bag. Just loose in his pants like pocket change. He took 'em. All of them. Must've been ten pills there. Then the junkie bitch came downstairs a few minutes later and she was just as high as Ant. And she was pregnant! Looked like a fucking swollen tick."

Annie Smallwood, though taking the Xanax, was on something different: heroin. She'd shot up in the past, had her first child removed because of her problems with the drug, and had, for a time, been off smack. No longer. She was a month and a half from her due date and shooting up daily.

> Darkness. Long streets, all winding,
> Shadows. Long nights, all unwinding.
> There is no Truth. There is no Light.
> —From the notebooks of Homer Antumbra

Annie Smallwood overdosed two weeks before she was due to have the baby. The couple had refused to find out the sex of the child but upon her admittance to Mercy St. Vincent hospital in downtown Toledo, Antumbra was told that his daughter was showing no signs of life. Smallwood was in a coma. There was talk of rushing her into an emergency cesarean section but it was abandoned as Smallwood remained unconscious and the threat of killing her with anesthesia loomed large.

She remained in a coma for three days. Her stomach was pumped. She was given Naloxone to counteract the overdose and she eventually pulled through. The child did not.

"He [Antumbra] called me in pieces," Steinbeck said. "He said she'd [Smallwood] overdosed and the child died. He said his daughter was still in her but there was no signs of life from the child. He said the doctors were waiting on Annie to have the child vaginally. Like nothing was the matter. I couldn't imagine what he was going through."

"We went out as soon as we heard. Drove the 700 miles in nine hours," Fulkers said. "We got to the hospital and Annie was still out—in a coma, like some television soap opera drama. She looked so frail and destroyed. The baby bump looked like a tumor. I guess that's probably because Ant had said the girl had died. Abigail, he called her. Broke my fucking heart."

When Smallwood regained consciousness, she was induced and delivered Abigail Rose Antumbra, who was indeed deceased. Social services were called into the situation but charges were not filed against Smallwood. I guess the loss of a child was deemed punishment enough.

> *She was so small, so sweet. Looked like she was just sleeping. They let me hold her. They wrapped her up in a little pink blanket and I nestled her to my chest and looked down into Abi's little quiet face. I almost believed that she was just sleeping. I ran my fingers along the contour of her little arms and hands, tried to gently tickle her, wake her. She wasn't there.*
> —From the notebooks of Homer Antumbra

"I don't know where he went. He came out of the room after Annie delivered the baby and just walked right by and out of the hospital," Fulkers said. "I chased him out into the parking lot but he wouldn't say a word. His face was white, like a ghost. He looked awful. He wouldn't answer me so I just let him be. I knew he needed to be alone. He just walked. I have no idea where he went."

No one saw or heard from Homer Antumbra for almost a month. He left his cell phone at the hospital and did not have a vehicle.

"I thought he was dead. I thought he went out and jumped into the Maumee River or something. I mean, he was crushed," Fulkers said. "I called and called and Annie finally answered and said that his phone was at the hospital. He just left it there. He didn't go home. He didn't show up in Minneapolis. He just vanished. It was terrifying. Really, really scary."

There are notebook entries during this time but they are mostly incoherent. Homer's handwriting is nearly illegible and there are stains—grass, dirt, mud, tears, alcohol, stains of all kinds—on the pages. The notebook itself seemed to have been dunked into water or left out in a heavy rain at some point.

There is next to nothing known of where or how Antumbra spent his 'lost' month. I've scoured the upper middle-west looking for arrest reports or hospitalizations but came up empty handed. When I asked him about it years later, he refused to answer me or talk about Annie or Abigail Rose.

"He just walked into the store," Walters said. "I can't remember how long it'd been since anybody had heard from him. I kept waiting on the phone call telling me Ant had turned up dead."

"What did he look like? Where did he say he'd been?" I asked.

"He looked like hell. Absolute hell. His eyes were sunken in, like a skull. Had these thick purple bags hanging under his eyes," he said. "He looked like he lost fifty pounds. Emaciated. Sick. He wouldn't talk about where he'd been. He wouldn't talk about Abigail, his little girl, or Annie. He just shook his head and his face got hard. He said he was ready to go back to work. I took that as meaning he was ready to go back on tour. I made the phone calls and started booking it immediately."

Chapter Eleven
Eventualities, Finalities

"Hershey called me up and said Ant had walked in and said he was ready to go on tour," Steinbeck said. "I was shocked. I thought he was dead or strung out somewhere. I rushed out of Louie's, where I was working behind the bar, and headed straight there [Glow-In-The-Dark-Skeleton Records]. He looked like a goddamn ghost, so skinny, so pale. He smelled awful and was dirty. I just wrapped my arms around him and cried."

Homer Antumbra and the band started practicing and writing new songs. Walters got to work scheduling a two-week tour, just to get the band back in the throes of tour life. But things were not like they were. Antumbra was a drastically different person than he had been before the loss of his daughter.

"The songs were heavy, droning epics," Fulkers said of the five song *remains* EP that came from the period. "Ant was writing these heavy meditations, through the eyes of the Dark River Chronicle's main character, Will. We didn't talk about when this bit occurred in the overall story but, from the themes, I'm thinking it was definitely a continuation of the *aworldofdarkness* record. They were about the meaninglessness of trying. 'Why try, the Way is a lie,' he sang. It broke my heart all over again because I knew these [songs] were, though veiled as part of the earlier albums, about Ant and his daughter. The songs were a portrait of the guy right there, right then, where he was, standing, shivering alone in the dark forsaking any sense of goodness, not believing it ever existed."

"Those were hard, hard songs to write and play," Steinbeck said. "They were about his daughter and his life, how he felt it wasn't worth living. I was hoping the work would pull him out of it. The grind, we called it. Back to the grind. But it was never the same. It was personal in a way, like a wound. Like his fucking heart was showing through his ribcage and he no longer cared to protect it."

The label released the album on black vinyl only, a major change from the multicolored releases of the earlier works.

"He said black only. I said that the kids loved the colored records but he wasn't having it," Walters said. "I said 'Okay, Ant. Whatever you say' and released it like he wanted."

The album sold well but not as well as the other releases. Several critics had similar arguments against the EP that were said about *aworldofdarkness*. The themes were in stark comparison to those related in his notebook entries and the songs he was working on prior to Annie's overdose. The themes of *remains* were the loss of innocence and a world completely and irrevocably corrupt. A sole comforting notion is that, while placing the album in the Dark River context might have been a way to deal with issues related to Annie's overdose and the loss of Abigail Rose, it's also relevant that Antumbra put the songs in the context of the darkest album in the Chronicles knowing that Will would again reach for and seek the Light. Maybe Homer Antumbra too would eventually reach for the Light.

The album was finished quickly; the songs were written and record-ed mostly simultaneously in Studio Eh. It was rushed to the plant and pressed in time for the band to take several hundred copies with them when they embarked on a Midwest tour a month later. The band did not return to Toledo.

News of Antumbra's daughter's death was not made public knowledge in the world of indie music. It was known by the band and several people close to the musicians but it was kept to that. Antumbra busied himself on tour with massive amounts of writing and drinking and prescription drug abuse. The band's performances were intense. I caught the Louisville show, but it was very apparent Homer Antumbra was under the influence. He was confrontational with any off-stage banter. He refused to speak to interviewers, critics or reporters, sending his band to answer any questions. He drank continuously during the band's performances and when he returned to the stage for the encore, his eyes were glazed and he focused more on his guitar work than any vocalizations.

"It was rough," Fulkers said. "Ant was popping Xanax from sunup to sundown. I think the only time I saw him with his eyes closed was when he nodded off. He didn't sleep like a normal person. He drank and took the pills until he passed out. That was his sleep cy-cle."

"Did you try and talk to him about his drug use?" I asked.

"Of course. I tried but it was like talking to a skeleton," he said. "He didn't even deign a response necessarily. He was going to do it and didn't feel defending himself or his drug use necessary. He just picked up the bottle of Old Grandad and drank deep then passed the bottle on to me."

When the tour ended, Homer Antumbra disappeared again. This time he set up shop in a small, crummy basement apartment with his guitar and his four-track recorder and recorded an entire album with no other musician accompaniment. There is no mention to characters or locales from the Dark River Chronicles. This was entirely an Antumbra album. He played guitar and keyboard and sang. The overdubs were sparse, only a vocal harmony here and there, and a brief lead solo on the keys or guitar.

"Eleven songs of anguish," Walters said. "That's what I heard. He didn't tell anybody what he was working on. He just vanished and emerged two months later with eleven songs of anguish. They were rough mixes, demos really, and I wanted him to let the band listen to them and then go into Studio Eh and cut some cleaner mixes but Ant wasn't having it. He said 'it's done' and upon further listens I think he was right. The mixes are ghostly, you can hear the creaking of the chair he was sitting on, the sliding of his fingers down the fretboard on the strings, the bumps of the people in the building above him. It was like listening to the specter in the attic."

"I was hurt at first," Steinbeck said.

"Because the album was so harsh?" I asked.

"No, because he didn't come to us with those songs," she said. "I was hurt at first but the more I listened to it, the more I realized that it had to be that way. That was his, you know? We would've just been a distraction. Sometimes it's hard to stare the Truth in the face but you have to. Ant used to say that. *flickersinthenight* was exactly like that."

Glow-In-The-Dark-Skeleton Records released the album, *flickersinthenight*, closely on the heels of the *remains* EP but it still sold well. Antumbra met with Walters and told him to set up a solo tour for him to support the album.

"He said he wanted to do everything on his own. He wanted to drive the van, play the shows, set up the merch table, sell the records, and drive on to the next date. All on his own," Walters said. "I had reservations to say the least. He looked like hell, pure hell. He kept getting skinnier. You'd think that would make the skin seem taut but it looked like it just hung from his bones. It was disgusting. Like a hairless cat or something weird. But he was adamant and I set the thing up. Three weeks. All alone. I felt like the warden sending him off to solitary."

> "flickersinthenight *is haunting. I don't know how to describe it any other way. It's spellbinding. Whereas some of the earlier songs could be seen as something of protection spells, this new work is like the embracing of black magic."*
> —Mark Jason's review in *MSD Review*

> "*The sparse arrangement has never been in more counterpoint to the dark lyricism. With the Dark River Chronicles there were moments of hope, searches for the Light. With* flickers, *all is forsaken. The thing should be inscribed with Dante's warning:* All hope abandon ye who enter here."
> —Staff review in *Few Horizons*

No lyrics were included with the physical release of *flickersinthenight*. The packaging was every bit as sparse as the recording itself: equal parts heavy silence and heartbreak. The cover was a cardstock print of a black and blue Antumbra painting of a decrepit leafless willow. There is no mention that it is a Homer Antumbra album nor is the title listed on the front. You have to flip the thing over to see the artist name, title, and tracklisting. I'm not sure if the songs were ever rehearsed or if Antumbra simply hit the record button on his four-track and laid bare his soul.

There is an exception, a solitary moment on the album where

there is another voice singing. Despite their rocky relationship, despite the loss of their daughter, despite their prolonged separation, at some point in the making of *flickersinthenight*, Homer and Annie got together again. They shared what would be their last moment together in Antumbra's basement apartment when Annie sang one verse and accompanied Homer on the choruses of "Rotted." The song is a series of mantras sung in a heavy, echoing dirge. Annie's verse, probably written by Antumbra, reads: "There is no Light. There is no hope. There is no tomorrow."

The two meet up and harmonize in the breathy, near whispering chorus: "Don't hope. Don't cry. Don't seek."

The fuzzy recording ends in an audible gasp or hiccup from Annie then the click of the STOP button being smashed down.

There are no lyrics or song notes for the song in any of his notebooks nor did any of the songs make their way into his performances in the ensuing tour, which would prove to be his last.

"He played on his own. Just him and his guitar. No backing band. He didn't play anything from his previous albums. He didn't even play anything from his newest. I don't know where the songs came from. It was crazy," Sonya Grimes said of the Cincinnati show during the *flickersinthenight* tour.

I met Sonya several years prior to this last tour at an independent journalist convention in Louisville. We both shared a profound appreciation of Homer Antumbra's art. I couldn't make it to the Cincinnati show but she took several videos and photos, which she sent to me afterwards. In the videos, Homer Antumbra stood swaying in the dim light before the microphone with his eyes wide but unseeing. He looked like a scarecrow fending off crows with his music. I didn't recognize a single song he played in the hour-long set.

"I think he was making them up as he went," she said. "It was absolutely insane. They were all so different, so intrinsic and it's hard to believe that he might not have worked out any of it beforehand."

After speaking to Sonya, I caught the Louisville show. I carefully studied the videos she sent me and listened for these new new songs, so new that they didn't even grace the newest Antumbra release, but didn't hear any of them either. Nor did he play anything previously recorded. A part of me wanted to believe that Homer Antumbra had entered into a highly creative period of his life, reminiscent of Dylan in the '60s, but his appearance spoke of something more profound and haunting happening to the man. That being said, he did not falter, he did not stutter, the songs seemed every bit as strong as the others . . . just different. Fundamentally different. They were structured but less so than anything previously released. They were often sprawling epics, circling lines peeling from the murk to embrace a solitary hook in less than expected places.

Mark Jason of *MSD Review* caught the Indianapolis show and had this to say: "He [Antumbra] put on a spellbinding performance. Pure, living, breathing avant-garde poetry in the flesh."

The Memphis independent music magazine *These Folks* called the shows akin to "viewing the somnambulist in the waking nightmare." The magazine also said Antumbra "seemed a man possessed, both of a living hell and a plethora of talent."

Others were not as keen on the performances.

"Gone were the songs of old. Gone were the songs of new. What kind of promotion was this? Does he think he's above giving the paying fans some semblance of a normal concert? Something they can enjoy instead of something they must 'experience', something too tough to swallow and only for the high-browed?" wrote Simon Balask in his online blog, *Cataracted Society*.

He continued, "Homer Antumbra highlights a major problem with the 'alternative' music genre. He holds himself above and beyond what he is: a working musician. He seems to think he is better than the average singer. He doesn't have to conform to playing the songs the people paid to hear. He doesn't have to give them something as lowly as a 'good time'. He can stand up there and act like he's communing with the great muse and broadcasting his special and unique music and we should, lest we are neanderthals, praise him highly and throw our dollars at the recordings of the songs he doesn't deem worthy of playing for us."

"I tried to get him to let me go with him, even if he wouldn't let me play," Fulkers said. "I told him I'd set up the merch table and sell the shirts and the records so he could focus on the shows but he turned me down flat out. Just shook his head and stared me down. Said he had to do this alone. It really hurt and he wouldn't explain any further."

"I caught the Indianapolis show," Steinbeck said. "He looked like shit. Absolute shit. But he looked possessed up there. Like Ant was gone and some other Ant from, like, a parallel universe or some shit, was up there and showing me the logical conclusion of his life. It was heavy."

"Did you talk to him about the songs he played?" I asked.

"I tried," she said. "I asked him where they came from and he said they came from where they always came from and left it at that. I asked him why he wasn't playing anything off *flickers* and he just shrugged his shoulders. He asked if I had anything, I told him no, and that was pretty much the conclusion of that conversation."

"Drugs, you mean?"

"Yeah."

After the Louisville performance, I spoke with Homer Antumbra backstage. I had emailed him letting him know I was going to be in attendance and would love to chat after the show and he left word with the venue to allow me backstage. I was taken aback at his appearance up close. He looked bad from the crowd but as I sat on the dingy couch next to him, I could see sallow skin, the cracked lines and pockmarks all over his face. His skin hung loosely under his chin. He looked awful.

"How've you been?" I asked.

His eyes looked like wet marbles pitted in the pale dried purple of the rotting prunes of bags hanging on his face. His glasses were scratched beyond belief. I don't know how he even saw out of them.

"The Way is hard," he said.

He seemed restless, unfocused. His eyes wandered about the room, his hands twitching in his lap, pulling a thread here, scratching an itch there.

A heavy silence hung around him. I didn't think I could penetrate it. I tried to get him talking.

"What have you been reading?" I asked.

His eyes turned to me and I saw nothing there. It was like looking into the empty reflection of a person. He was completely closed off. *Closed for the night*, the sign of his face read.

I didn't get anything much out of him. I thanked him for talking to me and asked him to keep in touch and let him be. I left the venue with an overall sense of foreboding. Something terrible was happening to Homer. He wasn't putting on a performance, as Simon Balask would have you think. He was lost, adrift, floundering. I hoped that he would find his way.

Chapter Twelve
Flickering Out

Little did I, or any of his bandmates or friends, know that Homer Antumbra was suffering from myriad severe, undiagnosed and untreated mental illnesses, including dementia and schizophrenia. The whirlwind of the solitary three-week tour exacerbated and highlighted the growing gap between what was real and what Antumbra perceived to be real. His notebook entries had several excellent and heartbreaking examples.

> *She's there. I know she is. Waiting. He is too. I can make out the wolf's eyes and gleaming teeth in the crowd. I must tell the Truth. I must Shine the Light regardless. I know they are biding their time though. Waiting to strike. I will pass into the night soon.*
> —From Homer Antumbra's diary

> *The bus creaks. The seat conforms to my bones. Take me. Take me wherever you're going. It matters not. I know he's behind me. I know only I can see his true face, the wolf's head, the glowing eyes, the pointed teeth, the*

A.S. Coomer

licking of his lips. Come what may, just hurry.
—From Homer Antumbra's diary

There are also several reports of strange behavior during the tour. Several shows almost didn't happen because of emotional crises in the back rooms of the bars or venues in which Antumbra swore there were people in the audience plotting to kill him when he took the stage. The Little Rock show was postponed a day when Homer showed up on the Greyhound bus wasted and paranoid. He stumbled into the venue and threw up whiskey and semi-dissolved blue pills all over the place. He refused to take the stage because "She's out there. She's out there and she knows I'm a liar. She's come for me."

When he arrived back in the Twin Cities after the tour, his friends and former bandmates hardly recognized Antumbra. All said he looked like "a corpse" or "a ghost" or "a dead man walking." All said he was nearly incoherent most of the time, fleeting moments of lucidity coming days apart and tinged with deep depression. He took prescription drugs—obtained on the streets—from the moment he woke, washing them down with an omnipresent bottle of bourbon or vodka of the cheapest variety, until unconsciousness took him. He did not have a place of his own but instead bounced between his friends and, often, slept on the streets leaving his guitar with Hershey Walters or one of his former bandmates.

It's truly amazing that Antumbra didn't miss any shows and was able to function at all, with the combination of mental illness and substance abuse, during the three-week tour. Especially in the light of the diagnoses he was about to receive.

"It was scary, seeing him like that," Steinbeck said. "Not just because of the drugs or booze. He wasn't right, you know? He was talking all this nonsense. People were out to get him. He wouldn't look you in the eye. Wouldn't sit still. He slept on the fucking streets. Like a hobo.

"I told him he could crash at my place whenever he wanted and he would start the night there sometimes. But when I woke in the morning he'd be gone and the front door would be standing wide fucking open. It was infuriating and so sad at the same time."

"I tried to sit him down and talk to him about what was happening to him," Fulkers said. "He wasn't there. Something was happening to his psyche and he was so out of touch with himself and the world around him that he couldn't see it. We tried a mini-intervention. Me, Skip, Steiner and Mikey. We cornered him at Hershey's and each told him how much we cared about him, how much we loved him and how worried we were and all that but it was like a wall or a curtain hung over his eyes and ears. He didn't see us. He didn't hear us. He wasn't there."

"It really makes you question things," Stephen Michael Harold Jr. said.

"What kinds of things?" I asked.

"Everything. What was the Truth, what was the Way, the Path?" he said. "What was real and what was fantasy? Was he delusional the whole time? Was what we were a part of nothing but contributing to the lunacy of a drug-addled schizophrenic? For me, it all came crashing to a drastic halt. I took a big step back. Moved back home then, after a time, re-enrolled in grad school."

"What do you think of it all now [after Homer Antumbra's passing]?" I asked.

Stephen 'Mikey' 'Specs' Harold Jr. paused for a long time before he answered. He had a hesitant way of speaking, slow and methodical, carefully etching the words together. When he spoke, his voice was level but his words were heavy with emotion.

"I want to believe we were a part of something greater. That the Path was real. The Light *is* real," he said. "I want to believe that's what we were seeking and that's what it all still means."

"He called me from jail," Steinbeck said. "I hadn't seen him in weeks, since he got back from that last tour. He wasn't making any sense but he somehow remembered my number and called me with his *one phone call*. I could hear the others in the background, 'Fuck this' and all that, and I was really scared for him. He had no business being there. He wasn't right, you know?"

"What happened?" I asked.

"I drove downtown and found out that they picked him up wandering around downtown, saying he was drunk, arrested him for PI. But when I talked to him he wasn't drunk, or high. He was just fucked up. He was out of his head. Bonkers. Ant wasn't there. I told the police that he needed help but they wouldn't listen. They thought I was just trying to get him outta the intoxication charge."

"He got the shit beat out of him in jail," Walters said. "He told some guy in there that he could see his real face, that he had a bear's head or wolf's head or something crazy, and the guy, he was a black guy, thought Ant was a racist and beat him senseless."

"He had to have reconstructive surgery, his jaw was broken so badly," Fulkers said. "At the hospital, they realized how out of it Ant really was. They gave him some mental tests and he must've failed them because he didn't go back to jail. They committed him to the psych ward upstairs then after a few days he was committed to Greystone."

Hospital records show that Antumbra was placed under an involuntary psychiatric hold then deemed mentally unstable and committed to Greystone Psychiatric Hospital, some fifteen miles outside Minneapolis. He underwent a battery of tests and a slew of diagnoses before the doctors finally settled on dementia and schizophrenia. He lived out the rest of his short life behind the impending slate walls of the institution, visited only by myself, Angela Steinbeck, and Brandon Fulkers.

My interviews with Homer Antumbra at Greystone were varied and circular. He was heavily medicated and even during the few—very, very few—moments of lucidity he circumvented all questions with cryptic musings on the Light, the Way, the Path, etc. Visits felt like confusing pilgrimages to some abandoned temple to speak with an ailing prophet, somebody you weren't quite sure was giving you sage advice or rambling on purposelessly because their hamster was no longer on the wheel.

Fulkers had brought Antumbra his guitar early on in his hospitalization but he largely ignored it. His focus was too limited for such things. He surrounded himself with books and magazines, though I don't think he ever read more than a sentence or two from anything he picked up. He wandered aimlessly through the halls and was the cause of several alarms during his short stay.

"Has a way with getting out, that one does," the nurse tech said during one visit. "A real Houdini."

I want to believe my visits made his time easier. A familiar face, along with those of Steinbeck and Fulkers, hopefully came as pleasant surprises. But I have my doubts. Though sometimes cheerful enough, Antumbra's memory at this point in his illness, was shot. I had to explain who I was on nearly every visit and he often looked confused and bewildered when I asked him about things he'd done or songs he'd written, people from his life. That being said, he often spoke of Will and Abigail.

"You know she buried him when she found him," Homer Antumbra said, his eyes dazed and focusing off into the sunlight through the clouded and dirty window in his small, cramped room.

"Who?" I asked.

"Abi. She was out to get some water for the wine and found him there. Like a drowned cherub," he said. "He was blue in death but she thought his face looked so peaceful, finally at rest."

It took me a second, as all of this came out of left field, but I realized that he was talking about Will, the character he created at the center of the Dark River Chronicles, and the beautiful woman in white that found his body and buried him. Apparently, she was Abigail Rose, his daughter that never drew a breath of life outside Annie Smallwood's drug-riddled womb. I didn't know what to say, so, I didn't say anything.

"Flowers came right out of it, you know?" he said. "The Light sometimes Shines of its own accord."

Homer Antumbra died on March 22, 2012 at the age of 39. Complications related to dementia and schizophrenia were listed as the cause of his death.

Homer Antumbra lived an embattled life. He fought the Darkness. He fought to Shine his Light, to see the Light. He strove to tell the Truth, walk the Path, the Way. Upon his death, his name, possessions, and finances became the hotbed for embattlement too.

I first spoke with Annie Smallwood the day after Homer's death. She called me saying that she heard I was a big fan of his and that she had some things she thought I might be interested in. I told her that I was, indeed, a big fan and was thinking about writing a biography on the man and his work. We set up a meeting to occur after his funeral in two days' time, at the small cemetery attached to the grounds of Greystone.

The funeral was a small affair, consisting of just the hospital's pastor, Antumbra's Greystone doctor, Brandon Fulkers, Annie Smallwood, and myself. Fulkers said Angela Steinbeck had planned on attending but had too bad of a hangover to make it.

"I thought she'd stopped drinking," I told him. "That's the way she made it out to me when I spoke with her."

"That's what I thought too," he said, frowning.

It was a short service. The wind whipped across the well-kept graveyard. Clouds swept across the gray sky and the pine box containing Homer Antumbra's withered remains was lowered into the hole dug for him. There was no headstone as of yet. Hershey Walters, upon prodding from myself and Steinbeck and Fulkers, had decided to get one made and it hadn't been ready in time for the funeral service.

I had something written that I planned on reading but when the small man in the black coat asked if anybody had anything they would like to share or say about Homer, I couldn't find my voice. It didn't feel right. I kept my mouth closed and, after a few more minutes, everyone moved away from the gravesite and the two men in gray jumpers picked up their shovels and set about filling in the hole above the casket.

I walked Annie Smallwood back to her car after speaking briefly with Brandon Fulkers. She was fidgety, dry-eyed, and obviously high. She was very skinny. She looked frail, elderly almost, deep wrinkles lining her eyes and mouth. She took out her keys and opened her trunk. I couldn't help but notice deep lines of grime on and under her fingernails.

She was rambling on about how she was very glad I was going to write a book on Ant and how she wanted nothing more than to be a part of it. She said I could interview her whenever I needed to and she would be honest and tell it all.

Inside the battered Subaru's trunk was an equally shabby wooden trunk. It had a few Glow-In-The-Dark-Skeleton Records stickers as well as a few for some bands and other labels on it. Annie Smallwood said the trunk had belonged to Ant and that it contained all of his notebooks. She said there were also songbooks and sheets of songs he wrote but never got around to recording: songs nobody has ever heard except for her and some that even she hadn't heard.

She said she needed some money and was willing to sell me the trunk since she knew I was working on a book about Ant and would take good care of his stuff. I hadn't yet committed fully to the idea of writing a biography but the fan in me was overtaken by what sat there before my eyes. I opened the trunk, ignoring Annie's chatter about needing the money to fight a case or some such dribble, and marveled at how many notebooks were stuffed inside the thing. I picked the first one up and skimmed. It definitely wasn't anything Annie Smallwood would've been capable of forging.

I offered her one hundred dollars for it.

She haggled for more and we settled on something closer to two hundred, everything I had on me.

I set about the contents of the trunk like a kid with a trash bag full of Halloween candy. I pored through the notebooks, one after another, until I had, at the least, set my eyes on every word, every song, complete or partial, every poem, every doodle, all of it. It took me days. When I was done, I felt I had something of an indie music holy grail. Something big must come from this, this treasure trove of genius. I set about cataloguing the material.

That battered, stickered trunk contained 67 full-size and completely filled notebooks, 15 smaller notepads, 206 loose sheets, 12 oil pastel works and 17 oil paintings. 703 songs and song ideas were in the notebooks and loose sheets of paper, 73 were complete; all of which had never been recorded or even played live, as far as I could tell. Fifteen of the completed songs were set in the Dark River Chronicles.

I rewatched the footage from the *flickersinthenight* tour and again wondered where those songs came from. I didn't find a trace of them in the trunk.

My first reaction, after carefully combing through the trunk, was to call Annie Smallwood and thank her. I even thought about sending her a few extra bucks. That's how excited I was.

I didn't call her nor did I send her any extra money. After all, a deal is a deal.

I called Hershey Walters and told him about what I had purchased from Annie Smallwood. He was ecstatic and told me to bring the trunk on over to the Glow-In-The-Dark-Skeleton storefront. He started speaking as excitedly as I felt upon discovering the thing. He said he had a new guy on the roster that he couldn't wait to get the songs to. Walters said he thought it would really set off the new guy's career.

He just assumed I was going to give him the trunk and all of its contents.

All of this gave me pause. I had this great musical history sitting on my living room floor and Hershey Walters wanted to use it as a springboard to get another big seller for his label. It felt wrong. I asked Walters if he and Homer Antumbra had a contract of any sort. The long pause after my question told me everything I needed to know. I politely informed Hershey that I would not be handing over Antumbra's notebooks. The rest of the conversation doesn't warrant printing.

I called Angela Steinbeck and Brandon Fulkers to tell them about what I had. Both drove down to my house in Kentucky for a weekend spent delving into the material. It was an emotional two and a half days. We laughed, we cried, we shouted 'Holy Shit!' but mostly we read, them for the first time, me for the umpteenth, with quiet, gaping mouths of astonishment.

We decided we had to protect this from Hershey Walters and anybody else that only wanted to profit from it. The stuff was too important. It was during this discussion that the idea of having a project lined up in the vein of *The Lost Notebooks of Hank Williams* or the *Mermaid Avenue* records came up. Though largely, and very unfortunately, not known to the mainstream media, Homer Antumbra's music was heralded by the underground. I've heard his songs covered live by several independent artists, not to mention the iconic Johnny Cash.

Fulkers and Steinbeck loved the idea and we set about making phone calls and sending emails to all the artists we thought would fit best on the album. I'm proud to say the thing is actually in the works. I'm not allowed to discuss it in detail as of this time, it's not a done deal as of yet, but I can tell you three major artists have already recorded and sent the masters of their versions of five of Homer's unreleased songs. Three more artists are on board and are either in the studio cutting their versions now or in the process of reworking them to fit their needs. We're thinking it's going to be called *Shining the Light: the songs of Homer Antumbra*.

It will not be on Glow-In-The-Dark-Skeleton Records.

In the past few months, while I've been tirelessly working on this book and the *Shining the Light* record, several ugly matters have come to a head. Annie Smallwood caught wind of the project and called me wanting more money. When I refused she sicced her lawyers on me, suing for a ludicrous amount of money for the trunk and its contents as well a major cut of any future royalties. She's claiming, or so her lawyers have told my lawyer (a friend from my undergraduate days), that she had a hand in writing those songs, whether by lending moral support to Homer or by actually helping *write* the lyrics. I like my chances in this battle.

I'm not the only person Annie Smallwood has deemed worthy of suing either. Hershey Walters, who in the wake of Homer's death garishly reissued all of Antumbra's recordings (removing all of the original artwork and replacing it with a headshot of the artist himself, something Walters himself knew Homer would never go for), is also being sued for royalties, past, present, and future.

The reissues themselves are a travesty when compared to the originals. Antumbra's entire discography was released on Glow-In-The-Dark-Skeleton Records and each release has been reissued without any of the original artwork or liner notes. The new liner notes were written by Hershey Walters and are laughable. In the liner notes to the *rage* EP, Walters claimed to have been in the studio with the band (which all of the band members have denied) and to have changed the directions of several of the songs to get them into their final states.

And Annie Smallwood didn't stop there. It seems she had a son in the time following the loss of Abigail. She claimed the child to be Homer Antumbra's. She sued for royalties, past, present and future, on behalf of the child as well. This case, I'm pleased to report, has come to a conclusion. DNA proved the child not to be Antumbra's. Smallwood's timeframe also didn't match up regarding the child's conception and birth and her last visit with Homer. She claimed the child was conceived while Antumbra was committed to Greystone. The hospital kept strict and detailed visitor logs and her name did not appear once. Also, some of Antumbra's medical issues at the time made the conception a near impossibility.

Annie Smallwood isn't the only person to sue for royalties though. Keith Skees and Steven 'County Fair' Williams have both sued for copyright infringement and royalties. Skees claims to have helped write several songs on *blackblacktheskywasblack*. Williams claims to have written several off that album as well as all the arrangements for the cover songs on *thesesongsiforgot*. I think these claims are dubious at best, the pitiful work of scavengers at worst. We'll have to see how they play out in court.

The last of the legal ugliness comes in the form of some extended family members also lawyering up and suing for royalties. I learned of this just last week and the details are sketchy at present.

A.S. Coomer

It appears that some second or possibly third cousins are suing for royalties but it is unsure on what grounds.

I've heard, though I have no physical proof at the time of writing this, that Hershey Walters has been in talks with several insurance companies and even a fragrance company in regard to selling several of Homer Antumbra's songs to be used in television commercials. I hope these rumors prove unfounded but at this point I wouldn't put it past Hershey Walters.

Epilogue

The legacy of Homer Antumbra's music will be long lived. Like Nick Drake and countless others who were largely unknown during their lifetimes, Antumbra's music will come to be known for the genius inherent in it. Every note, every word, every dripping, static silence was meticulously placed. Everything in Antumbra's music serves a purpose. The songs and albums are a reflection of the midnightland so many of us find ourselves living in day after day. It's a dark pool reflecting just how hard life often is.

His music is more than the ramblings of a madman. The songs are more than just the blather of an alcoholic or pill head. Homer Antumbra, like so many of us, was not a static being. He was in a constant state of flux. Through life, we all find ourselves doing things we never thought we would, things we never thought we were capable of, good or ill. We all become things we'd never expected to become. That's the beauty and the beast of it. Plan though you might, life has a way of working its own will into nearly everything you set up. The music of Homer Antumbra reflects this. We seek the Light, the good. We try to Shine the Light and do no harm. But the Way is Hard, Shadows and Darkness obscure what, in retrospect, should be clear, obvious choices. That's the way of things.

The music, the teachings of Homer Antumbra, show us that the road to Hell is paved with good intentions. Everybody is trying to do the best for themselves, trying to do what they think is right. There is a Light and there is a Darkness but there is the in-between world, the midnightland, where things are often muddled and we're unsure what we need; what we want even becomes difficult to distinguish. The most we can hope for is to Shine our Light while it glows. Reach out and show the Way whenever we find it.

Writing these last few sentences, Antumbra singing softly in the background, the quiet understanding of "Last Breeze" from *aplaceinthelight*, tears brim my eyes. I guess this is the feeling so many neophytes have upon conversion. This is the wanting to share something so beautiful, so enormous, so full of Truth and Hope and Sadness and Light and Darkness, so full of All, with the world at large. Though you won't find me on the street corner chanting, "Hare Hare Antumbra Krishna", I hope this small, simple book goes a long way in spreading the Truth and Understanding of Homer Antumbra's work.

> *I've made the flame*
> *I'll shine my feeble light*
> *Waving it towards the shadows*
> *In the dark and windy night.*
> *May this be enough,*
> *For the breadth of momentary illumination,*
> *However brief,*
> *May this be enough.*
> —From "Feeble" from *blackblacktheskywasblack*

Appendix

Discography

Homer Antumbra had a total of sixteen releases during his lifetime: nine LPs and seven EPs. Inside the parentheses following the title of each release is the number corresponding to its release order, e.g., *blackblacktheskywasblack* was Antumbra's first release so in the parentheses following the title is the number 1, as it was released first.

Full-Length Albums

1. *blackblacktheskywasblack* (1)
2. *whatwillcomewillcome* (3)
3. *midnightland* (9)
4. *aworldofdarkness* (10)
5. *darkwaters* (11)
6. *steppingfromthedarkness* (12)
7. *returning* (13)
8. *aplaceinthelight* (14)
9. *flickersinthenight* (15)

EPs

1. *thesesongsiforgot* (2)
2. *acceptance* (4)
3. *rage* (5)
4. *autumnalhymns* (6)
5. *pathwaysoflight&darkness* (7)
6. *ladyatthecrossroads* (8)
7. *remains* (16)

A.S. Coomer wrote *Rush's Deal* (Hammer & Anvil Books/Lit Fest Press), *The Fetishists* (Grindhouse Press), *The Devil's Gospel* (The Wild Rose Press), and *Shining the Light* (Atlatl Press).

www.ascoomer.com

Other **Atlatl Press** Books

Failure As a Way of Life by Andersen Prunty

Hold for Release Until the End of the World

by C.V. Hunt

Die Empty by Kirk Jones

Mud Season by Justin Grimbol

Death Metal Epic (Book Two: Goat Song Sacrifice)

by Dean Swinford

Come Home, We Love You Still by Justin Grimbol

We Did Everything Wrong by C.V. Hunt

Squirm With Me by Andersen Prunty

Hard Bodies by Justin Grimbol

Arafat Mountain by Mike Kleine

Drinking Until Morning by Justin Grimbol

Thanks For Ruining My Life by C.V. Hunt

Death Metal Epic (Book One: The Inverted Katabasis)

by Dean Swinford

Fill the Grand Canyon and Live Forever by Andersen Prunty

Mastodon Farm by Mike Kleine

Fuckness by Andersen Prunty

Losing the Light by Brian Cartwright

They Had Goat Heads by D. Harlan Wilson

The Beard by Andersen Prunty